SOMETHING
MUST BE DONE

by

DORA BEALE POLK

.

HONNO FICTION

Published by Honno
'Alisa Craig', Heol y Cawl, Dinas Powys
South Glamorgan, Wales, CF6 4AH

First Impression 2003

© *Dora Beale Polk 2003*

ISBN 1 870206 56 8

British Library Cataloguing in Publication Data

Published with the financial support of the Arts Council of Wales

Cover design by Debbie Maidment

Typeset and printed in Wales by
Gwasg Dinefwr, Llandybïe

Dora Beale Polk was born in Pontnewydd, Monmouthshire and went to school in Pontypool. She was at college in Cardiff during World War II, taught English, and was very active in the Labour party. She moved to Colorado for a year, married and has lived in America ever since, though she comes back to Britain every year. She taught Celtic Studies at the University of California and was Emeritus Professor at California State University. She is been active in Democratic politics. Her previous published work include *Hiraeth*, *Mari Llwyd* and *Vernon Watkins*.

ACKNOWLEDGEMENTS

Grateful acknowledgement is made of financial support from the Arts Council of Wales for publication of this work and a grant from the California State University Emeriti and Retired Faculty Association in the final creative phase.

An illuminating critique by the Welsh Books Council and the expert editorial assistance of Janet Thomas are greatly appreciated. Thanks are also extended to Joan Bellamy Melman, William Millinship and Olga Beale for their help and advice. Especially valued are the vision and enterprise of the founders and developers of Honno Welsh Women's Press.

I would like to stress that this is a work of fiction and no resemblance to any actual individual or institution is intended or implied.

CHAPTER 1

As a girl I used to worry what I'd say if I, Davidia Williams, had to swear on the witness stand to tell nothing but the truth. I already knew back then that it isn't what you know, but when and how you know it that you have to watch. And sometimes the hardest job is to separate fact and fantasy. But I do know this: none of this would have happened if my father hadn't had this weird fancy that he was connected to the Prince of Wales.

Certainly without this harebrained "mumpy", as my mother used to call it, he wouldn't have got his fine Welsh nose bloodied and broken. It was still in sticking plaster on December 11 1936, when King Edward VIII renounced the throne.

When the six o'clock news reported that His Majesty's Declaration of Abdication Bill had received the Royal Assent at 1.52 that afternoon, my father leapt up like a madman from his tea and rushed headlong from the house.

My mother lashed out after him, "If you're going where I think you're going –" she meant the taproom of the Pontbran British Legion Club – "to get like last night –" she meant drunk – "don't bother to come back." She sourly observed to me, "You would swear that it was him who was giving up the throne, and not the thundering King. It is out of all proportion the way your Dad have been behaving, Vid, over something that don't make one shred of difference to the likes of him."

"That's what *you* think, Our Mam," I felt like answering her back. I had not turned fourteen at that time, but I could have told her nibs a thing or two – if I hadn't been sworn to secrecy.

My father was sober when he came back several hours later. We were subdued to silence by one glance at his grim face. Ignoring everyone, he stretched behind his chair and switched on the wireless to warm it up. As luck would have it, the battery had been recharged the day before the crisis broke. He waited, sitting ramrod stiff, staring straight in front of him. If you discounted his taped nose, in side view he resembled the severe picture of the King broadcasting his first message to the Empire the previous St. David's Day.

The Westminster clock on the sideboard in the middle kitchen thrummed its on-the-hour, four-phrase chime and started to strike ten. My father swiveled violently to turn up the volume. Leonard Hasty, my sister Muriel's most persistent suitor after Angelo, consulted his Great Western Railway watch. "That clock is nearly half a minute fast," he said.

"It's as near to right as dammit is to cursing," said my mother.

Using his favourite catchphrase to retreat, Leonard said, "Well, there it is."

After that, the only sound in our back-kitchen was of hot coals shifting gently in the grate. I got the feeling that everything and everybody, everywhere, had stopped to listen. It was like the two-minute silence at eleven o'clock on Poppy Day. More silent yet than that.

"This is Windsor Castle." The voice was gruff. "His Royal Highness Prince Edward." At least one tantalizing question – what they would call an abdicated king – was solved.

An awkward bumping sound came from the linen and fretwork face of the loudspeaker, followed by an empty pause. Then came the crisp staccato voice we had heard so many times before. The Prince of Wales was in the kitchen with us.

"At long last I am able to say a few words of my own. I have never wanted to withhold anything, but until now it has not been constitutionally possible for me to speak."

My father's lips compressed in bitterness.

"A few hours ago I discharged my last duty as King and Emperor. And now that I have been succeeded by my brother, the Duke of York, my first words must be to declare my allegiance to him. This I do with all my heart."

My father's face took on a yellowish cast. It was a sickly echo of King Edward's summer bronze, acquired on his August Adriatic cruise, but sadly faded by the time he came to see us in South Wales. Less than a month before, that was, and already a pained memory.

"You all know the reasons which have impelled me to renounce the throne. But I want you to understand that in making up my mind I did not forget the country or the Empire which as Prince of Wales, and lately as King, I have for twenty-five years tried to serve."

Even the crepey bags under my father's eyes looked like the King's, the latter's a result, his enemies whispered, of debauchery, but perhaps caused, it now seemed, by strain.

"But you must believe me when I tell you I have found it impossible to carry the heavy burden of responsibility, and to discharge my duties as King as *I* would wish to do, without the help and support of the woman I love."

My father fiddled with the plaster on his nose to hide his face. But my mother put her top front teeth against her lower lip and blew, to show "woman I love" meant Jezebel.

"And I want you to know that the decision I have made has been mine and mine alone. This was a thing I had to judge entirely for myself. The other person most nearly concerned has tried up to the last to persuade me to take a different course. I have made this, the most serious decision of my life, only upon the single thought of what would in the end be best for all. This decision has been made less difficult for me by the sure knowledge that my brother with his long training in the public affairs of this country, and with his fine qualities, will be able to take my place forthwith, without interruption or injury to the life and progress of the Empire. And he has one matchless blessing enjoyed by so many of you and not bestowed on me, a happy home with wife and children."

At this my sister could not quell the sob that bubbled in her throat. Leonard turned beet red, as though embarrassed by so public a display. "During these hard days I have been comforted by Her Majesty, my mother –" my mother's flaring nostrils revealed compassion for Queen Mother Mary in this awful hour – "and my family, the Ministers of the Crown, and in particular, Mr. Baldwin, the Prime Minister, have always treated me with full consideration. There have never been any constitutional differences between me and them and between me and Parliament."

My father snorted in contempt of Baldwin's duping of the King. The saddest part, he'd said many times, was that the King never knew what struck him. If he'd stood his ground, what could they have done to him?

"Bred in the constitutional traditions of my father, I should never have allowed any such issues to arise. Ever since I was Prince of Wales, and later on when I occupied the throne, I have been treated with the greatest kindness by all classes of people wherever I have lived or journeyed throughout the Empire. For that I am very grateful."

Something in the Prince's timing told us he was working swiftly to his climax now. We all steeled ourselves for pathos and to hide our faces from the others.

"I now quit altogether public affairs and I lay down my burden." A horrid lump formed in my throat. Our Muriel stared hard in front of her, trying not to spill the rapidly-collecting tears down her cheeks. "It may be some time before I shall return to my native land, but I shall always follow the fortunes of the British race and Empire with profound interest, and if at any time in the future I can be found of service to His Majesty in a private station, I shall not fail.

"And now we all have a new King. I wish him and you, his people, happiness and prosperity with all my heart. God bless you all. God save the King." The crisp voice broke on a jarring note. The glass vase on the wireless vibrated sympathetically.

Now our Muriel wept unrestrainedly. She wept for a tragic ending to romance: that a king must choose between love and country when by rights he should have both.

My mother picked up the bottom of her pinny and dabbed her eyes. She stood where old Queen Mary stood: grieved for the suffering of the King, yet strongly believing in the harsh necessity of choice – the woman or the throne, preferably the throne; all for duty and respectability.

I knew how moved my father was. His face was hidden still, but I could tell the tears were running backwards down his nose by the way he rushed outside to hawk and blow.

He wasn't weeping for the passing of the King *as* king. He hadn't blinked an eye when that grand old gentlemen, King George the Fifth, had kicked the bucket the preceding January. Nor did he weep exclusively from a sense of personal loss of a "butty" who had shared the sickness and emptiness of war to become the symbol of a generation playing games with death and sure of nothing but uncertainty.

No. My poor old Dad was eating his heart out with guilt as well as grief. He was beside himself with self-reproach for having let his Sovereign down. He was convinced he and his comrades had thrown away the sole chance there had been to save the King.

Then, my lips were sealed. But in the lapse of many decades, the entire cast of that secret brush with destiny has quit the scene. Tich Veasey's recent death has now completed my release from my childhood pledge of secrecy.

Besides, it is high time to give Edward VIII his due. He deserves some sort of a rebuttal to the vicious charges leveled against him by insolent revisionists. The media often distort history till it has little resemblance to survivors' memories of the events.

What I remember best of 1936 is my father's insight that the King was hunted down and symbolically beheaded, without trial, by political executioners. The "unlawful marriage" issue was a last-straw pretext to do him in. The "constitutional principles", that a king cannot be both a king and his own man, were concoctions of his enemies. Even Labour got sucked in. By failing to defend the King's free choice of partner, they lost, for many years, the chance to serve the needs and yearnings of the common man.

This is the chronicle of how my father and his butties, in devotion to their Prince, came in touching range of fame – or infamy. It is their sole monument.

CHAPTER 2

If I had taken more after my mother, who liked to put in a good word for the Lord occasionally, I could start at the Creation and be sure to cover everything. I don't believe it would be overdoing it to go back in geologic time to when the South Wales coalfield was laid down. Our second-form Geoger book advised picturing the coal deposits as a meat dish heaped with mountains, the coal seams coming to the surface at the limestone rim. This formation, they said, had resulted in a compact economic unit of nine-hundred-odd square miles.

But coal wasn't all South Wales produced by any means. Indeed, the area's first large-scale industry was iron mining, and the coal was won originally only to smelt the ores. Then came the iron, steel and tin-plate manufacturing industries. The tin-plating process was founded in our valley in about 1670. The famous Thomas-Gilchrist improvement on the Bessemer steel process was made there in 1876. When local iron was depleted in the nineteenth century, the thriving iron, steel and tin-plate industry switched to imported ores.

Great waves of immigrants from other parts of Wales, from England and Ireland, swarmed into the region to man these industries. Their terraced homes were crammed along the steep sides of the many rivers gouging their way across the mountains roughly north to south to converge upon the ports of Newport, Cardiff and Swansea, further west. Along the narrow valley bottoms, colliery workings, blast furnaces, steel mills and tin-plate works, shops, roads, railways and canals competed for scarce room. But always up above, the mountains reared their bleak, wild humps. The slopes between the grimy troughs and the mountain moors radiated the redeeming loveliness of hill-farm cultivated fields, pastures, bracken patches and woods.

The way our land was made, the way it looks, bore directly on our lives. The exploitation and distribution of its economic wealth had everything to do with what my father felt and did regarding Edward VIII.

In terms of characters, this drama started on a summer evening in June, 1894, when a great-grandson of the aged Queen Victoria was born. The baby was a grandson of the Heir Apparent who would become Edward VII in the new century. The father of the baby, Edward's eldest son, would later become George V. The baby was sovereign-royal through and through.

The babe's official name when he was christened in July was Edward Albert Christian, followed by the names of patron saints of England, Scotland, Ireland, Wales: George, Andrew, Patrick, David.

Us sensitive Welsh regarded our precious name coming last as a spit in the eye, so I was told. It should by rights have been the first. For wouldn't this baby one day, as firstborn of a reigning monarch and Heir Apparent to the British throne, be invested as the Prince of *Wales*?

As luck would have it, not long afterwards, the royal babe's maternal grandmother succumbed, and the funeral wreath's inscription revealed that the family called him "David". It was marshmallow ointment to the sore-afflicted feelings of us Welsh. It also sat well with the pious and superstitious. Wasn't David King of Kings?

The day this child was born, an explosion at the Albion Colliery near Pontypridd, South Wales, killed 268 men and boys.

A few months after the birth of the royal prince, another boy was born – in an ancient terrace cottage in Pontbran. That industrial village lies in the easternmost valley of the South Wales coalfield where it meets the rolling farmland of the Usk. The Afon Llwyd, the Grey River, flowing through that valley, was scummed and sullied by the dross from many workings of the iron, steel and tin-plate industry.

The baby was called Frederick Edward. The first after his father, the second for the Prince. This baby was my father, Fred E. Williams.

The trivial connection of the close births of my father and the Prince was blown up out of all proportion by the Williamses. The jokers in the family even called them "twins". They based their banter on a physical resemblance of unspectacular coincidence of fair, curly hair and baby chubbiness.

The ragging went from "twins" to telescoping and confusing the two. Whenever a new picture of the little Prince was published, they would rib, "Here's our Fred again. He ent half popular."

There were pictures published of the royal toddler in lace-and-cambric frocks. As a boy they had him snapped in sailor's suits and highland sporraned tartan kilts. In adolescence, photographs and portraits showed him decked in ceremonial outfits. In one, he received the Royal Order of the Garter at Windsor Castle on White Rose Day, the day before he turned seventeen. Another showed him at his father George V's coronation shortly afterwards.

"Where do you keep your wings to, our Fred?" the family would twit.

"Not wings, mun; aeroplane," another wag would carry it along.

"Whatever, he don't half get around. Windsor, London,

Ireland, Wales. All within a fortnight. Quite a gadabout he is."

"And what a toff in all them fancy rig-outs. It's a wonder he ent too stuck up to live with us."

It was a Williams family trait to get so infatuated with a bit of homegrown wit they would drive it into the ground. The marvel was that my father didn't hate the Prince from getting sick to death of being teased.

Early photos of my father do indeed reveal a marked resemblance to the Prince. Especially with them both in Eton collars, and, later, khaki uniform. The blond hair, the slight, wiry body, not very tall. Even the features: the straight brow and natural frown, the outline and the closure of the lips.

When I was growing up, a lot of people kidded us we were "The Royal Family". Not (obviously) because there was the vaguest parallel as families went, but just because my father and the Prince were lookalikes.

I can only speculate when my father started to feel personally close to his beloved Prince. Perhaps it was when his Royal Highness was invested as the nineteenth Prince of Wales: the relish and excitement that my father put into the telling and retelling of that scene years after the event gave it the aura of a fairy tale.

"There is this beautiful castle of Caernavon," he would tell me. Maybe we were catching snails or picking apples. "It has these thirteen towers. Some daft people think thirteen to be unlucky. I have always found it otherwise. Don't trust to everything you hear, Vid. A lot of it is superstition. Well, the towers are hexagonal. Which is to say six-sided, look. Now you remember that, Vid," he would admonish me.

"Hexagonal, six-sided. It is education, mind.

"No, nobody is living in the castle now. It is called a noble ruin. Similar to Newport's, only bigger, with fine lawns around. A moat, too. And these little turrets."

Here he was liable to work in bonus stories of mediaeval knights raising the drawbridge and lowering the portcullis. He'd put archers in the lookouts and would himself pour boiling water on the English from the battlements.

When I got him on the track again, he would continue, "There was this platform, see, between the Black Tower and another. And up above was the Welsh Dragon flying in the breeze. You can bet Lloyd George had seen to that. Here comes the Prince in his velvet coat and snow-white britches. Which only princes can afford to wear, the seat gets soiled so fast.

"Then his Dad, the new King George just crowned, decked out in admiral's duds, invested him. Which in plain English means gave him the crimson velvet Cloak and Mantle. And put the Coronet of gold upon his head. Then he gave him Sword and Ring and Rod. The Ring went on his middle finger to make him husband, look, to Wales, and father to her children. Then next he did his homage to the King, and sat down on the Third Throne while Mr. Churchill said his piece." He'd pause here to fill me in on Churchill's politics, contrasting him with Lloyd George, the great Welsh Prime Minister of the Great War years.

Resuming potting bulbs or cutting cabbage, he'd go on, "The Prince spoke lovely in reply. Even said a bit in Welsh: 'All Wales is a sea of song.' Not just his title, says he, but his name bound him to Wales. David like in your name, Vid." That's when the source of my ridiculous handle dawned on me.

Sorting through a bunch of family memorabilia in my early teens, I came across a souvenir copy of the *Western Mail* commemorating the Investiture. The paper boasted three pages of "live" pictures, a considerable journalistic feat in 1911. Remembering certain high-flown phrases my father used, I realized that he must have got the whole experience secondhand. He had long since made it all his own, however. I doubt if he knew where imagination had taken over from reality.

He always ended the account, "That is how my double came to be sworn in." By "double" it was clear that he meant more than parallels of looks, or of character and temperament. He implied a mystic bond going deeper than the surface.

Shared horror and the common suffering of war fanned my father's sense of close affinity with the young Prince, though actual correspondences between their wartime lots were practically nil. My father served in the ill-starred Dardanelles campaign. He was one of the "poor mugginses" who fought the last trench action on Gallipoli against the Turks. He was among the last to swim to the evacuation ship in those cold January waters of the Hellespont. The Prince did not participate in that soul-shrivelling experience.

"Regular bloody pity, that," my father said. "He would have found a hell of a lot to bear out his suspicions about some bloody people's damn stupidity. How small they value human life. Other poor buggers' than their own, that is."

My father never doubted the Prince's *personal* wish to go into that deadly sphere. Had not the Prince pleaded with Lord Kitchener to be allowed to go to war? "If I die, there are my brothers to succeed me," the Prince was reported to have said. When they finally permitted him to go to France, he led the generals so merry a dance by sneaking to the Front that he left my father in no doubt that he would have won a VC if they'd given him a chance to show his stuff.

Instead the Prince used the opportunity to extend his comradeship towards the common man. He played football with the Tommies in the Flanders' mud and rubbed shoulders with all sorts.

"He made you feel he wanted nothing better than to be

like us," my father was fond of telling me. "Still, they were quite right to hold him back. Him being something extra special, they dared not risk him falling in the enemy's hands. To die was one thing. To be taken prisoner another. Think what a powerful club the Germans would have held if they'd taken the British Heir Apparent hostage. We'd never rest, mun, till we got him back. Our whole morale depended on him being safe."

Later, I was to remember that remark when my father had to make a decision similar to Lord Kitchener's.

After the war, the Prince's and my father's lives more spectacularly parted company. While the Prince gallivanted round the globe, a bachelor ambassador, my father took my mother, Gladys Harris, to the altar soon after he got back in mufti and settled down. They had barely warmed their rented house in 15, Pantygasseg Place, Pontbran, when they found themselves proud parents of my sister Muriel. And a few years later, in 1923, to be exact, I came into the world to disappoint their fondest hopes.

Slated to be their dearly beloved son with the long-chosen and inevitable appellation of David Williams, I turned out to be a girl. Whereupon, in an act of unmatched silliness, they encumbered me for life with a made-up, feminine equivalent.

My father's unrequited yearning for a son may have been more responsible for my cocky independence, than my natural bent. For he treated me with the confidence and freedom reserved for boys, rather than the kind of patronage that was then usually applied to girls. As his hopes for a male heir grew dimmer, I enjoyed more and more the status of the son I should have been.

He confided to me once in a mood of soft regret, "There was supposed to be another nipper in between our Mu and you." But he failed to make it on the team. Later, in my teens, another such event was scheduled but got scratched. For which my mother thanked her Maker for sparing her indecency.

One reason that the Prince was in no rush to marry was the limitation of his choice. The European royal families were getting bowled out one by one, and the royal marriage market was in low supply.

My mother, greatly taken with the royal doings, used to speculate with aunts and friends whom he would end up marrying. Would he take a commoner to wife – which meant an aristocrat, I could never fathom why. The families of the royal blood were so inbred, it wouldn't be a bad idea. There'd been too much intermarriage between the offshoots of old Queen Victoria. For one reputed to be so Victorian, she had been enormously prolific.

If my father got drawn into the conversation, he'd maintain, "Stands to bloody reason he ent gonna let them dictate who the hell he'll marry. Nor he ent the sort to have the bigotry to only marry royalty. He'll please hisself, wed some nice 'oman who he loves. Or not at all."

Unfurling the tablecloth, whipping it sharply to get it laid across, my mother said, "You have consulted with him personally about this matter?"

"Damn right, I have. I only got to look into my own mind, mun, to know the way that chap do think."

"Would it be degrading to your Royal Highness to kindly pull that corner of the table cloth down straight?"

"Gorstruth! The Prince ent half smart staying single, mun." He winked to me that he was only having her on. "No taking on a pack of trouble with a loud-mouthed bitch. Not like us stupid buggers, daft enough to let ourselves get hooked."

"I couldn't agree more!" my mother huffed, meaning the "stupid" and the "daft" he had just called himself.

Even as a child I knew in my marrowbones my father's identifying with the Prince of Wales was not like the wishful thinking of a schoolkid for a cinema star. The pauper pitied rather than envied his princely counterpart. I can hear him saying it now, "You wouldn't catch me changing places with that poor old sod for all the jewels in the blinking tower. They make his life a misery. Do this, do that. Cock your bleeding finger when you hold your cuppa cha. Don't sneeze or else you'll shift your blwmin' crown down round yer eyes. If he tried to pick his nose, they'd slash his bleedin' hands off in a jiffy. My heart goes out to him. The chap ent built to stand that sort of bloody nonsense no more'n me."

When my mother and sister gushed over the little charmer, Princess Elizabeth, the Duke and Duchess of York's daughter, and wished they could have frocks and trips like her, my father would say, "Aih! Get away! The nobs can have their flaming pleasures and their palaces. Good luck to them. I'd rather have it comfy here with my two kids and my old dutch, muddling along in my old tinpot way." Then, saucering his tea and blowing on it, or sopping up gravy with a piece of bread, he'd add, "No having to watch my blwmin' p's and q's. Afraid to belch when you feel the need. You'd go off your head trying to bottle it all up."

"Oh, Fred, there's crude you are," my mother chided. "And in front of our Vid. She'll be repeating it outside and be my death of shame." My mother didn't know me very well. Quite early on, I had learned the difference between what was private talk and what was free. I already had two codes of manners, and two languages, coarse dialect and proper standard English. I tried hard to apply my mother's bourgeois standards to teachers, preachers and the like. The rest of the time I was myself, my father's son he never had.

My father's sense of psychic kinship with the Prince was the more remarkable since he disapproved of royalty on general principles. If my father had lived a generation or so earlier, when the British Crown was in danger of toppling after Victoria's days, he would undoubtedly have been a staunch supporter of the Republican Club Movement.

Yet this bizarre contradiction in his thinking had an odd parallel in his regal counterpart. It was well known that the Prince was no ordinary specimen of royalty. By some quirk in his personality, he did not himself enthusiastically support the monarchy, nor blindly accept the authority of other established institutions like the Church. Growing up, he had rebelled against his stuffy elders and their ridiculous traditions. If he had to be of royal rank, he wished they'd let him be like his Scandinavian relatives who walked casually in the streets among the crowd. He hated sham and humbug. His independence and unconventionality went deep. The teeming, nimble ideas of the New World attracted him, and he adored the vital, young Dominions and anti-royalist America. Open to brand-new ideas, he saw nothing as ordained or inevitable, and was mightily disturbed about the economic mess that plagued the country. He felt an obligation to connect with the downtrodden, and had the ready gift of making spontaneous contact with them when the Establishment allowed him to get close.

The Prince was the very stuff republicans are made of. He was my father all over again. Like two peas in a pod were that democratic king-to-be and that prince-loving anti-monarchist working man; head and tail of the same sterling coin. There never was a quainter spectacle than a flaming radical defending a hereditary overlord who was himself a rebel to the bone.

Could anything ever come of this odd affinity?

CHAPTER 3
1923 TO 1929

No connection, but the year I was born was our region's last year of prosperity. While I went through the nappies, rubber pants and dummy stage, the coal industry began its downhill trot. By the time I moved up from the pram into the push-chair, the miners, sick of government failure to solve the coal crisis, went out on strike. The General Strike of 1926 was called in sympathy.

Characteristically, while the upper classes decried the "irresponsibility of the masses", the Prince donated to the Miners' Fund. "Strictly a nominal contribution," according to my father. "Ten pounds or summat. More to give the miners heart than anything. But the stink the bigwigs made, you would have thought it was the annual revenues from all the Crown Lands put together.

"Yet, far from criticising him, them top dogs should have ought to gone down on their bended knees to him for acting as a safety valve. If it wasn't that *we* knew the Prince knew we deserved a better hand for having spilt our guts out on the battlefield, we'd have broken into armed rebellion. After all we went through in the war, dirt was his thanks as it was ours."

Somewhere in this period, my father hatched a special variant of what in pidgin Welsh my mother called his "mumpy". In Welsh *mympwy* denotes a whim, obsession, a bee in one's bonnet, a spider in one's attic. A smattering of bastard Welsh and some funny Celtic constructions still salt the speech of us Anglo-Welsh, alienated from our culture since the Act of Union of 1536 made English the official language.

So came this new twist in my father's mumpy: the Prince should be recruited as official leader of the working man.

His memory of how this came about was rather vague, as in this exchange at the supper table. "Didn't I say back then, Glad, how they ought to put the Prince on the Trades Union General Council?"

"I never heard you saying such a thing," my mother said.

"Well, at least I said he should be voted honorary Chairman of the Miners Union for his nice dib-in-the-fist to them."

"Ooh, Fred Williams. There's a fibber."

"You can't deny I said he ought to represent the colliers on another Coal Commission with more guts or . . . summat . . . of the sort . . ."

My mother gave him one of her straight looks.

He shot back, "All right then, woman. What *did* I bloody say then, since you're so clever at remembering?"

"The most I ever heard you say was something potty like you wished you were a dickey bird to fly down on his shoulder and whisper in his ear."

My first recollection of hearing anything with my own ears was on Christmas evening in 1928. My Granddad beckoned to my father to leave the parlour. They went in the kitchen to share the earphones. The Prince was to make a speech over the crystal set. He had come back prematurely from a tour of Africa to help his father in his illness.

While they juggled with the squealing, crackling earphones, beaming at each other like a pair of fools, I drew pictures in the window-steam, thick from cooking and the frost outside. I drew a scooter Father Christmas had omitted to "put in my stocking". That venerable character wasn't all he was cracked up to be. He practiced favouritism. I got fleece-lined knickers and a useless doll. Willful, wayward, rude Tich Veasey got a tricycle.

When the speech was over, my mother came in to quiz. She gathered up peel, nutshells and pulled-cracker scraps to justify her presence. She said, "What did he have to say then?"

"Appealing for the Lord Mayor of London's Fund for tiding over miners in distress," my Granddad said.

"It's more than tiding over they do want, mun," said my father. "Neville Chamberlain admitted it. A lot of unemployment in the collieries is permanent. So what price charity? The Prince might just as well have saved his flaming breath."

With theatrical astonishment, my mother turned around from flashing up the fire with the party litter. "Why, Fred! I never thought I'd live to hear you criticize your blessed Prince."

"It isn't him, poor bugger. He tries his best. He's just a cat's paw for the bloody government."

"What's catspaw, our Dad?" I said.

Slowly his face unfolded from his tizzy. He encouraged me to ask him questions, so it stood to reason I'd be bound to blow some of his lather off occasionally, and he always took it in good part.

He mimed the story of the monkey duping the cat to pull nuts out of the fire. He shot out his arm and pincered his hand an inch short of the blaze. "The government's the monkey, the Prince is the cat. But it's not nuts, it's clinkers they are making him pull out. They have nearly doused the fire of British industry."

Suddenly his blue eyes kindled. "Why can't we make him *our* cat's paw?"

My tiny, black-frocked grandmother appeared. "Good gracious me! What's that you said?"

"No, no, Mam. Nothing mean. I only thought to get the

chap to speak for our side for a change. Which is a hell of a sight nearer to his heart than them. Get him to go on the wireless like tomorrow, Boxing Day, and say, 'This is the workers' turn. The miners reckon charity ent what they want, but rights, rights, rights, to a bloody decent job. Now this ent politics, mind, listeners,' he'd say. 'Fair's fair, this is just to even matters up, to give their side of it like I done yesterday for Mr. Baldwin and his lot.'"

My uncles Bill and Jack came out to hear my father waxing eloquent. They clapped and hear-heared, and declared he ought to put up for the council. They all enthusiastically approved the mumpy.

What, I came to wonder, did the coal depression and miners' charities have to do with us? My father was no workless collier. He was a cog in the tin-plate industry, specifically a furnace man. He had worked his way up from a mill hand to that skilled position. It was all he knew besides odd-jobbing and his beloved hobby, gardening.

We had never wanted for the decencies of life. We had four square meals a day, at least as much as I could pack away of bread and "taties", if a bit light on the meat. There was a nice big fire always in the kitchen grate, a grey slate roof over my head in a "modern" six-room red brick terrace house, and a cosy millpuff bed in the little back bedroom aired by the kitchen flue. I had warm clothes on my back and stout boots on my feet.

Sometimes I was made conscious of these blessings by my mother's harping on my failure to appreciate my luck. From time to time the dirty kids in school, with running sores and impetigo scabs around their mouths, ringworm in their scalps, nits in their hair and "heat-bumps" on their arms and legs where fleas or bedbugs welted them, got boots and old clothes handed out to them from charities. It made me feel a cut above to be ineligible. I hadn't yet experienced the nasty jolt of knowing others were comparing themselves down to me. Until this knockback to my pride, I shared my father's blithe enjoyment of his lot. For, funnily enough, although he struggled for a bigger piece of the economic pie, he never let it spoil his wholesale relish of the crumbs he got.

But, bit by bit as I grew older, I began to understand that my father's interest in the welfare of the miners was not entirely selfless. He was sharp to realize that if one part of the economy was sinking, sooner or later the other parts would cave in after it. By that holiday season 1928-29, declining tin-plate orders had already meant "short time" for him. It was works' policy that a full complement of skilled workers should be kept on tap for a fast return to full production whenever the time came. The owners preferred to close the works a couple of days a week than to reduce the labour force. The Union approved this allocation of scarce work, but my father scorned its premise. "There ent gonna *be* no getting back to full production unless we get a Labour government in fast."

A month or so into the New Year of 1929 it was bitter cold, with snow banked solidly beside the roads. It had been around so long, it was dirty at the edges. The canal had frozen every night for several weeks. Robin redbreasts had grown tame from want.

My father, my sister Muriel and I wrapped ourselves in scarves and knitted balaclavas and went up the bank to see if the ice was thick enough for playing on. All the other kids and dads in Pantygasseg Place had the same idea. We stamped around blowing through our gloves and cross-arm slapping while the fathers had a testing conference. It ended with a go-ahead.

I helped my father tie a pair of rusty skates onto his boots with rope. The leather straps had perished and gone green with mould from having hung up in the coalhouse many years.

Copping on to our antics later in the day, our Muriel had this to say, "There is a clown our Dad was! You should have seen him, our Mam! His ankles wobbling, then his feet shooting out from under him. And when he landed smack dab on his bum –" She couldn't finish for laughing.

She forgot, till I reminded her, to point out that at least he was no sissy like some other fathers there. They slid kitchen chairs in front of them or even used their kids to balance on.

I was one of the unlucky ones who fell in when the ice cracked. Though the water was no higher than my shoulders, that great assault of cutting cold petrified me. My flesh felt shrunk and trembling.

"It is the shock," my father soothed my bawling when he fished me out. "That water's cold enough to freeze the sphincter off a sphinx."

They took me home to get me out of my sopping clothes and warm me up with scalding tea.

Trying to deflect the blame, my father made excuses to my mother. "The whole bloody village crowded on to that bit of the canal in front of Pontbran Orchards pub, the stupid lot." He ignored the fact that he was one of them.

"Straight to bed for you, my girl," my mother said. Seeing me shivering and dripping puddles on her polished oilcloth, my woollies shrinking on my back, put her in a ratty mood. She made it sound as if the bed bit was for punishment.

"Oh, no, she ent doing nothing of the kind," my father said. "It wasn't her fault falling in. What she do need for throwing off a cold is keep the circulation going, hot up her blood. She shall dress up warm and dry and take a nice long hike with me."

Darned coms and stockings, last year's brown serge pinafore slip and an old coat of our Mu's were quickly rustled up for me. He took me out the country to Llanfrechfa. We struck across the frost-hard fields where the local minor gentry sometimes rode to hounds. On the way back, we dropped into the Upper Cocks to wet our whistles. He sat me on a bench in the warm bright passage outside the public bar, and brought me out a glass of pop. "It is shandy really," he stage-whispered, with an exaggerated screw-face wink, "only don't let on, it is against the law." He had poured a drop out of his pint of draft beer into the squash. "The ferment from the hops be just like medicine against the cold." My mother used the same excuse to take a teaspoonful of whisky in her tea.

Inside the public bar, if they weren't talking about the hero of the masses before my father put in an appearance, they were the minute afterwards. The subject was specifically the Prince's recent flying visit to the blighted areas in the north. Off his own bat, without pomp or ceremony, he had gone directly to the terrible slummy little rows of houses where the miners lived. He paid unexpected calls on despairing families who could not believe their eyes to see the Heir Apparent standing on their shabby doorstep asking to come in.

Through the crack I saw Obadiah Dixon with his elbow on the bar. "It wasn't for show. It was completely jonnuck. He even asked to see the grocery bills."

I heard Ted Swilling's voice, "Aye, and the pay sheets, mun."

My father said, "What if it had been South Wales he picked? Pontbran even!" He laughed deep in his chest, a pleasant rumble enticing you to follow suit. I did. Out there in the passage by myself.

"Can you imagine my old dutch answering his knock, mun?" he went on. "There's a stew she'd be in. She is bad enough when the relations land on us unexpected."

On our way home, my father was a good deal quieter than usual. He whistled softly through the spaces in his teeth, breaking off to humph and chuckle now and then. I knew he was communing with himself.

Returning through the village, we popped into Uncle Jack's. Uncle Jack was my father's elder brother. He was a roller on a different shift at the Rustbrook tin-plate works. He concealed a harelip with a shaggybrush moustache, yellow at the drooping tips from licking in his tea and beer. His wife, Aunt Rispa, gave off a smell of must like a Rider Haggard mummy. It was something of an ordeal to be hugged and kissed by them.

My father sat down at the kitchen table with Uncle Jack and repeated the discussion at the Upper Cocks. Aunt Rispa tried to shunt me off into a conversational siding about school and dolls, but I trained my main attention on the table talk.

"So what I have been thinking, Jack, is this," my father wound it up. "Why don't we try and get the Prince to come down *here*?"

"How, mun?" The air escaped through the cleavage in my uncle's palate to snuffle down his nose. It made a jumble of his words.

"How?" my father echoed witheringly. "How did he get to go up north? Exactly the same way."

"And how was that?"

"Hell, how do you suppose? Someone must have put it in his head that Durham was the place worst hit."

"Who though, and how?"

My father puffed hard on his cigarette, then drummed his short, blunt fingers on the yellow oilclothed table, spilling ash. "You know, Jack, what I think we ought to do? We ought to write."

"Who write?"

"We could get the British Legion Club to do it on behalf of all of us. Put a motion to the meeting. It would be fit, the Prince being British Legion National President."

"Who is our local secretary this year?"

"Ern Lippiatt."

"Gordam, he be a way too ignorant to write a Prince."

Playing sudden-thoughted, although I guessed he had been mulling it, my father said, "What's wrong with me to write it, then? If a cat can look at a king, a poor bugger like myself should ought to be allowed to drop the Prince a line or two. Though I says it myself that shouldn't, p'raps, I have got a tidy hand."

"But *you* ent out of work, Fred. Would it be quite right?"

"Nor ent the Prince. But that don't stop him *caring* how the poor sods in the bread lines and the soup kitchens are managing. All the more reason to give them a helping hand." He stubbed his cigarette. "Besides, the way that things are going, it won't be long before we're on the dole ourself."

That evening my father got out the pen and ink and a Woolworth's blue-lined writing pad from the sideboard cupboard. He had all of us to help, including Idris Llewellyn who lived with his auntie, Mrs. Llewellyn-next-door. It wasn't that Idris had any particular talent for the job. But since my father had had to call across the wall to borrow blotting paper, he had felt obliged to state the reason, and had consequently to invite him round. Besides, Idris always brought along a flagon of home-brewed stout that he was famous for in Pantygasseg Place.

The biggest hurdle was the proper form of salutation. There was nothing pertinent in *Arthur Mee's Encyclopedia* that they had bought on hire purchase for our Muriel and me. Nothing in the Davies's (next-door-the-down-side's) book on letter writing.

"Miss James would know," my mother said. Miss James was the teacher living in our street who gave us caste.

"Aw, shw't. En this the very thing the Prince don't give a damn about? As long as it is from the heart, he'll understand. I bet a tanner I am not the first old soldier to do this and make a muck of it. What shall us put? Dear Sir?"

Muriel was positive it should be "Dear Prince". My mother plumped for "Dear Royal Highness" and Idris diplomatically supported her – she had frowned on him for bringing in the drink.

Jokingly, my father said, "You might as well drop your opinion in the pot, our Vid."

"Well, en he *our* Prince, Dad?" I said.

My father understood me like a shot. "You mean our Prince of Wales! Ah, yes. Like rub it in. Out of the mouths of bloody babes."

Thereafter I was treated as an oracle resolving any conflict which arose until the following letter was produced:

> *15, Pantygasseg Place,*
> *Pontbran,*
> *Wales*

Our Dear Your Royal Highness The Prince of Wales:

Just a few lines to tell you how glad we are you are taking such an interest in the colliers, who are having such a hard time since the War. I am not myself a collier, but like you, are sorry for their plight. Also like you I am a member of the British Legion and a fellow ex-serviceman.

The reason I am writing this letter is to remind you that the South Wales area is as hard hit as the Durham area. Most of the colliers here are on the Dole. Some have not worked since my youngest girl was born. She is named Davidia after you. She is six years old.

The reason I am writing this letter is to ask you to come and see what the Welsh People are having to put up with. Your Own People, and Returned Soldiers a lot of them. I sincerely trust you will take no offence at me writing to you like this. It is because you are so well thought of among your ancient vales and mountains. We are all behind you here, and it would give us heart to see your pleasant smiling face, and welcome you into our homes, and sing God Bless the Prince of Wales.

Hoping to hear from you in the near future, I am your most obedient and humble servant,

Signed, Frederick Edward Williams.

He underlined the Edward to stress and seal the bond.

My mind got a big boost out of this experience. It was leaf mould for my brain. It felt like looking forward to Christmas, except that Christmas was a happening, whereas this was *doing* something to *make* something happen. My father's mumpy showed me the road to activism, and the excitement, anticipation and suspense that flowed from it.

Not long afterwards, my father got a most imposing letter through the post. He was at work when Arthur Hoare, the postman, dropped it through the letterbox. My mother lingered in the passage while she scrutinized the envelope, clearly of two minds to open it. She was so curious, she nearly went up in a puff of smoke. But she resisted the temptation to hold it in the kettle spout, pry the flap, and then reseal it with a flour-and-water paste, as I had sometimes seen her do.

"Run down the works and take this to your Dad," she said.

I ran. Faster than a hare in fright of being jugged. Down Park Place, beneath the railway span across the brook, and round the goods wagons standing in the sidings.

I ran not because I thought there was much need of

urgency. The chief spur was curiosity. I also loved to pay a visit to the works. It was an awesome place, full of great strange echoing roars and wondrous sights. There were flaming furnaces in which steel bar was heated dull red hot, whipped out with tongs, and slid across the shiny floor for passing through the rolling mills. Then back it went again for reheating and re-rolling into plates, doubling at each stage. Then on to other sections of the works for pickling, annealing, cold-rolling, annealing and pickling again. Till finally, the thin steel sheets were dipped and coated with the shiny, precious tin.

I explored the works from end to end at every opportunity. The noise-and-bustle was pure joy. Better than a carnival. I longed to wield a pair of giant tongs and tuck a steel bar in the corner of the glowing furnace like my father did, or do a rhythmic dance like Brynley Thomas's dad, passing the red hot metal strip back to the behinder, through the rolls, squeezing it like paste under a rolling pin. Or even be a pickler like Ted Swilling. Or all of them.

That was the world of real romance. A man's world where muscles rippled, skin glistened and even a little shrivel like poor Austen Bishop or an ugly gibbon like Tich Veasey's dad resembled Hercules in bronze. It made me sad and mad I was a girl.

My father's face split at the sight of me. He propped his tongs against the furnace wall and came towards me, rubbing his hands on his scorched duck apron. He mopped his forehead with the sweatcloth hung around his neck. "What's up?" he yelled above the clash and din of hissing, slamming, snipping metal.

I held out the letter. He looked alarmed. "Our Mam said fetch this down. It just come in the post."

He grabbed the snowy envelope and tore it open. Stained, work-callused fingers shook as he unfolded the rich parchment. As he read, a beaming smile replaced his anxious look. "I'm damned," he said. "There's nice." And to Ruby Jones's father and Bryn Thomas's father, who had just come up to slap my back and tousle me, he said, "Here mates. Read this." He gruffed his voice in order to tone down his pleasure, and not seem smug.

Bryn Thomas's father read aloud, "Dear Mr. Williams: Your kind letter has been received. Please rest assured the thoughtful suggestions it contains will be carefully considered. It is indeed our earnest hope that solutions to these problems may soon be found which will be fair and beneficial to all concerned, and will do no injury to either side. Yours very truly, Edward, Prince of Wales."

It was a better tonic for my father than a bottle of Parish's Food. He felt the good for days. He kept the letter with its elegant crest and magic, bona fide signature in his waistcoat pocket to exhibit on the slightest pretext.

When it began to get the worse for wear – the edges ragged, the folds worn through, the pearly margins marred by sweaty fingerprints – he made the big decision to preserve it for posterity in an ornate, gilded Woolworth's frame, and displayed it ever after on the front room mantelpiece.

Impatiently we waited for a drop-in visit from the Prince of Wales. Ordinarily my mother tended to be on the slap-dash side, but she stood in mortal terror that the Prince would catch her in her "dissables". So she took to organizing her routine in such a fashion that she was squared away by ten o'clock with her kiss-curls baked in shape and a clean pinny on.

I never saw her so methodical and houseproud. Spit and polish, brasses rubbed up once a week. The steps and porch kept scrubbed. And never a day went by but she brushed blacko on the bars and hobs and oven-door, and shone them up like jet.

It naturally went ill for me. She nagged me constantly to wipe my boots or hang my coat up on the hallstand. But Our Muriel got it worst. Being older, she was always having to dust down the stairs or put the mop over the floors. As for our Nip, a decrepit, dopey spaniel, my mother wouldn't let him set paw in the house. He led a dog's life like the rest of us.

It went so far, my father had to put a stop to it. One night, coming in off afternoons, I was woken by his bellowing, "Jesus Bloody Hurrah. Corned beef again, is it? You are getting very handy with the tin opener! When am I gointa get a decent meal under my bleeding belt again?"

My mother's voice whined up the chimney, "I am slaving my insides out as it is, Fred Williams. One pair of hands is all I've got."

"There's no need to neglect the stomach, though. Let some of the fuss and faddle go. This ent a damn museum we be living in."

"*You* are the one who wrote the Prince to come."

"Dear Christ. You still on that? Even if he came, you don't think for one minute he'd look in the corners, do you, Missus? As if he'd care a damn that there were cobwebs on the ceiling, or a bit of fluff behind the carpet rods. Besides, he probably have got a bit too much to do to come right now. What with his Dad not picking up after his operation as he should."

In later years, my father would end his reminiscence of this episode, "So that put an end to that jig for a bit. The old girl let her hair back down and henceforth wasted less time on the folderol and spent more time on the feed."

He made it sound easy to dismiss. But I had a budding intuition that disappointment merely fueled his mumpy to try other ways. What lark would he come up with next?

CHAPTER 4
1929 TO 1934

Spring, 1929, the canal teemed with tadpoles like currants in plum duff. The air reeked with the sickly scent of may-blough. At the polls, my father marked his ballot with a cross for Labour and helped to win a Lib-Lab victory.

He rejoiced. Now chronic unemployment would be licked.

But before we could look around, we heard more bad news. I gathered that hordes of humpty-dumpties in America had slumped from some high Wall into the Street. The crash that broke them resounded round the world.

I also had my own share of bad luck that autumn. I went up from the Infants into Standard 1. Till then, I had believed that Life was one long downhill breeze like sliding down the Slippery Path, a grassy, glass-smooth incline up where the heather and the harebells grew and where in late summer we went to pick the juicy purple whimberries for tarts.

But Miss Watkins leaned against the brass-railed fireguard, hogging the warmth with her broad-beamed behind, and warned us we were only at the bottom of an endless uphill pull. As spitballs disappear on a flatiron just drawn off the fire, some of the life-joy sizzled out of me, never to return.

For the next few years, against the worldwide horror of depression, my father felt as helpless as the rest. Prime Minister MacDonald's Labour Government went nowhere fast. "He is all mouth and no do," my father strafed as tin-plate working fell to half its plant capacity.

In the summer of 1931, the Labour Government announced it would make good on its election promise to aid the nation's black spots, blighted even before the general slump.

"They ought to get the Prince of Wales to spearhead it, Owen," my father said to a visiting cousin bright enough to be a student at Cardiff University. He was pale and thin, his pullover unravelling at the elbows. My father went on, "The Prince could fly down in his aeroplane. There is a nice flat field to land in up by the Siloam Chapel." Some outfit had come there the previous summer to show us our first aeroplane, giving joyrides at a bob a minute to the few who could afford the thrill.

"This isn't anything to spearhead, Uncle Fred. The government have only authorized a *study* by the University."

"The Prince went to Oxford!"

"Aye, aye. But this here is a drone's job, look." He was careful not to sound impatient. "A dry old business collecting the statistics from firms and Labour Exchanges." Owen was studying history and economics to go into politics. It had not occurred to me before that anyone could do that. I listened, fascinated, to everything he said.

"Statistics, is it? And what is to become of these statistics when they got them, eh?" my father demanded.

"Well, there you are! Bugger all, I wouldn't doubt. It is nothing but a gob-stopper to shut us up. In any case, it is too late." He was already bitter at nineteen.

"Too late, Owen?"

"This Government is doomed. They are borrowing in the millions. And who is going to bear the brunt? Us poor buggers. They are cutting the dole and sailors' pay. All to save the bloody bankers from, so-say, a collapse of currency."

A few weeks later we trembled at an unknown terror called National Bankruptcy. Labour Prime Minister MacDonald threw in his lot with the Conservatives and formed a "National" coalition government. The working man's last hopes went tumbling.

A little later, in the lovely tawny, copper autumn, with my father's famed chrysanthemums in bud and the mountains a sharp pencil line along the top of Mynydd Maen as far down as Twm Barlwm, the nation once again expressed its will. Baldwin's clever ploy to get a popular mandate for the "National Government" brought back a huge Conservative majority to Parliament.

The day following the election my mother sent me down the village to drop off her weekly grocery order at Pattimore's Caernarvon Stores. I also had to fetch some bones for stew. The Sunday joint would only stretch so far.

"Oh, yes, Vid," said my mother, "and call into Powell's for a mantle for the gas. Take care, now, how you carry it, it's delicate. On second thoughts, you better get it from the Ideal Stores. I have let old Powell's bill run up. Some change is on the meter I was keeping if the gas should go. No, p'raps you better take it from Aunt Jinny's teapot on the sideboard. Gibby the Milk will have to wait till next week if I'm short. Keep clear of Reese's. They will only call you in to send me up another bill. Duck below the sill as you go past. Mrs. Llewellyn-next-door would like a swede and some shallots from Evans the greengrocer's. Feel to see if they are firm."

Down the village I paraded, feeling silly, like an old woman, carrying the frail. As it bobbed against my legs, the rough straw caught the turndowns of the latest pair of socks knitted by my grandmother.

Scummy-lipped, unshaven men dawdled on street corners, hands hooked in trouser-tops or braces. Fishy-eyed and collarless, they cwpied on their haunches in their doorways, or loafed around the Oddfellows and Railway Inn. Some were without the wherewithal to go inside at opening time. Some had kept back a couple of shilling from their dole before they forked it over to their missuses. They were hardened against tongues which clacked, "Shocking, drinking up their benefits. It do suit some people not to do a stitch of work and let the government take care of them."

Inside the sawdust-sprinkled butcher's shop, bloody-stomached Mrs. Beak dispensed her chops and gossip. That day she turned from death, sin and disgrace, and who was in the family way, to post-election observations.

As she whacked the chopper, her breath escaped in little bellow-spurts, "Marvelous that people had the sense to put the Conservatives back in."

"Sense?" scoffed red-faced Percy Cook, a butty of my father's. "Stupid dullards don't know which side their bread is buttered on."

Mrs. Clem Jenkins said, "I wouldn't say that, Perce. Labour made a mess of it. It's only right to give the other side a try to pull us out."

"All due respect, but you have it all arse back'ards, Missus. It wasn't Labour made the muck, but that flaming sod MacDonald. And laugh! *You* have got him now. Labour have disowned the filthy turncoat."

"Language, language," Mrs. Beak said waggishly, wrapping sweetbreads in some newspaper, "and no talking politics in my shop, please!" although she'd been the one who started it.

My social life centred on the Rechabites, a friendly society to keep kids off the streets and out of pubs. They said they were for Temperance. In actual fact, they looked upon all alcohol as Devil's spit.

It was no great sacrifice for me to sign the pledge. They wouldn't let a girl of nine buy "strong waters" even if you had the money. Besides, I didn't much care for the taste of it. My father slipped me swigs of homemade elderberry wine experimentally. And once I nipped the whisky in the sideboard cupboard, which my mother imbibed as medicine to "loosen croup" and "build her blood". By count of tea-spoonfuls of whisky in her tea, she was a chronic invalid.

The leader of the Rechabites, crinkle-haired Nwd Probert, was a jolly, tolerant soul. But because we had no Temperance Hall, we had to meet in the Baptist vestry where they wouldn't let you dance. That wasn't any skin off my nose, but it chafed our Muriel. In later years, I had reason to be grateful to the Baptists for delaying her discovery of the joys of being in a fellow's arms.

The restriction on activity made it more a swapshop for ideas. Some of the things we talked about were worse than dancing by a long chalk. Not just naughty jokes, but Marxism and even Darwin's revolutionary theory. They would have put the pastor, Reverend Willie Spinum, as we called him, in a foaming fit, if he had known.

In the winter of 1931 to 32, although my own life was progressing well enough, I gathered the country was in turmoil over incomprehensible matters like "tariffs" and "The Gold Standard". I wished Owen was around to translate for me.

"What's tariff, mun?" I dared to ask an Abersychan High School bloke.

His nostrils flared as wide as adits. I slunk away. Later, it came to me he might be ignorant, and feigned disdain to save his face. Next time I'd ask somebody with the grace to say so if he didn't know.

"Tariff is charging foreigners a fee for selling stuff to us," Nwd said.

"There's daft. That don't make sense."

"Look at it like this. The Frenchies sell steel bar to your Dad's work to make tin-plate with. Now me, I'm making steel myself at Baldwin's."

"Why don't our Dad buy bar from you then, Mr. Probert?"

"Why, indeed. There's using your old noggin, lass. But the

Frenchies steel's a wee bit cheaper. We get better wages, see. Tariffs is to jack their prices up to ours. You following?"

"So then our Dad's works might as well buy steel from you?"

"Which is only right and proper, ent it, to patronize your own."

When my mother minded neighbour babes, she lullabied them with "Land of Hope and Glory" and "England's Green and Pleasant Land" patting out the rhythm on the little woolly-shawled cocoon, drumming it right in. So preference to home-manufactured steel versus the Frogmade stuff which came across the Channel sounded fair enough to me.

Teatime the next day, I raised the subject with my father. Being on night shift, he had just got up. That was my mistake. He often grizzled on arising; he was extra grumpy sleeping days. Milk, bakery and greengrocery carts and vans clanked and roared across the ruts of our front street. Us rowdy kids played marbles, knocking-up-ginger, tag and hopscotch. We screamed bloody murder when we fell in the canal, grazed our knees on filler-ashes in the lane, or got strapped for stealing ha'pennies off the mantelpiece. I should have known better than to rankle him. But I didn't realise the subject was so sensitive.

"Jesus Bloody Wept," he blazed. "That crafty bugger fills your head with bosh. I'm tin-plate. He be steel." Cups hanging on the dresser chinked.

"Kindly keep your voice down to a roar," my mother said, herself adding to the volume. "Lady Llewellyn may be hard of hearing, but she ent past feeling her foundations trembling."

My mother's pointy tongue only aggravated him the more. Misreading my bewilderment, he waved his fork and fumed, "Don't scowl at me, you little imp. I won't put up with it. I'll give you such a lamping –"

"Naih, mun, our Dad," I whined. "I am only puzzling. Isn't Nwd Probert in your Union?"

He swallowed what he had been fiercely masticating, and said more soberly, "Aye. But us tin-plate members in the little works be daggers drawn with our steel-making brethren over these here tariffs. It stands to reason *us* do better when our management can buy cheap foreign bar. If the government do slap the tariff on, *our* management won't be able to compete with the tin-plate made by the giant works. Then *I'll* be out of work."

His voice had dropped decidedly, so it must have been the unpleasant prophecy that set my mother off again. "I wish you two'd stop wrangling. I go to all the trouble to make pasties for your tea, and for all you know what you are eating, I could have dished up pobs."

"Naih, woman, it ent wrangling. Controversy is education, and the pasties be delicious. Dish me out another helping and don't interfere."

"You are encouraging that kid to grow into a troublemaker. I have got enough to do with her already, with her cheek, without you putting all these rash ideas in her head. Much more of it, and I will brain the little madam. A proper little tomboy she is turning out to be. Why isn't she like our Mu? I cannot fathom how two kids can be so different."

Our Muriel, their pride and joy, sat there as good as gold, being seen, not heard. Being seen was probably ample satisfaction for her – she made everybody's face light up, save mine.

As despising as I was of her, I could see she was a pretty piece of goods, with cheeks like polished pippins and eyes as deep blue as the Cwmglas reservoy. Her hair waved softly down in hanks of silver silk to end in lazy loops. She didn't have to twist it up in rags, or frizz it in the curling tongs that my mother kept handy on the hob for crimping her own rats-tails.

If I had cared about the things that most girls cared about, I couldn't have helped feeling envious of her. For *I* had the misfortune to take after my mother's chunky, chubby, non-descriptness with scant, mousy hair that could only be cut basin-style. In looks my sister bore a strong resemblance to our father. In temperament, however, they were as different as storm and shine. While he would blow his plug before you could look around to find out what was rumbling, she was the essence of sweet patience. They treated her as though she were the Kohinoor Diamond in Queen Mary's crown.

"Go on, baby her, see if I bloody care, bloody little white hen's chick," I said.

"There is the end!" My mother brought her fist down hard enough to bounce the cruet and tureen. "Bad language I won't tolerate." She made me wash my mouth out with carbolic soap, a token gesture, at the sink.

Even after I had paid my penance, she kept cribbing, "So help me I will break her before she is much older, or die in the attempt."

My father came to my defence. "Aw, knock if off, now Glad. Leave the kid alone. She's not the type to be your usual silly biddy, all frills and paint. She has a good head on her shoulders that she is learning how to use. Give her half a chance and she'll turn into a scholar, and be a credit to us both one of these days."

"All *I* hope is that she will turn into a lady." Her tone suggested that she thought her hope forlorn.

Winking at me round her back, my father said, "I don't think there's much danger she'll be that."

My father's mumpy took a slightly different twist in the years between 1932 and 1934.

My father knew the Prince was helpless to do anything directly to solve the nation's problems. Law and custom kept him – like all kings and princes back to the seventeenth

century – without political power of his own. A mere fig-
urehead. But the Government couldn't stop him using his
station to give the workers heart. He threw his weight behind
recreation schemes to provide the unemployed brief respite
from drear, poverty-ridden homes and spirit-sapping streets.
He was photographed visiting workers' settlements, impro-
visational community centres in stark barns with a few poor
sticks of furniture, a Union Jack, a picture of the King and
Queen, and a shelf of dilapidated books.

In the past, there had been new moon grins and waving
arms to welcome him. Now he was received only with
solemn, sour faces and limply hanging hands.

"Stinking bloody lot," my father said. "They don't deserve
the Prince's sympathy."

But Obie Dixon said, "They are fed up, Fred, with all the
hypocrisy and cant. They have been fooled long enough by
a ruling caste. You can't blame them refusing any longer to
be taken in."

"But it ent the Prince's fault, poor bugger. However down
they feel, it wouldn't hurt them to show the fellow a bit of
hip-hip-hooray to speed him on."

For if, my father argued, working men desired the Prince's
backing, they had a duty to reciprocate. This was a principle
which, little did he know, would form his desperate last
defence of his dear Prince a few years hence.

So now, out popped his mumpy in its obverse form. "Hey,
mates, how about trying again to fetch him here? Not for
him to cheer *us* up but for us to buck *him* up a bit. It would
do his eye good to see us jolly, pally bunch."

"Take him down the British Legion, is it, for a good booze-
up?" Tich Veasey's father said exultantly. Like Tich, he wasn't
overstocked on sense.

"Well, no, I don't suppose that would be proper. But –"
he brightened – "we could rent the Welfare Hall, since that's
the sort of place he likes to go."

"Put on a damn great beanfeast for him," Ted Swilling said.

"Peas, taters, brussels sprouts from our allotments."

"My old 'oman's pickled beets and cabbage."

Said Idris, "And I'll make up a special batch of stout."

"I hate to put the damper on," Obie Dixon said, "but he visits Welfare Halls only to see people getting culture there. Us lot hardly set foot in the place, except to get the dole."

During the day, the Hall served as the local office of the Labour Exchange. Long lines of men wound around, both inside and outside the walls, to sign up twice a week. Black, spotty faces, hunch-backed by coal-dust-coated lungs, coughing and gurgling. White, coarse-grained faces like lumpy porridge, from excessive sweating in the works. Faces as red and netted with fine purple lines as chronic drinkers', but from furnace burn.

In the dressing rooms behind the stage went would-be mothers, or mothers with squalling babes to have them weighed and get free cod liver oil and powdered milk.

Only in the evening did culture reign. Nwd Probert went to Male Voice Choir there. Ted Swilling dabbled in amateur theatricals and the annual operetta. But the creative outlet of the rest ran mostly to no more than the tending of their gardens and allotments – plots of land allotted by local governments to keep the workless busy and their saucepans filled.

"The Prince is just as much behind allotment schemes as Welfare Halls and Workmen's Clubs," my father said. "Wouldn't it be just as nice to invite him down to hoe a row with us? Then stop and rest, smell the flowers, have a smoke and a good old gas? It cuts both ways, you know. If we give him *our* confidence, make him feel that he is one of us, he'll give us his."

But he was only just-supposing. Would his mumpy ever get beyond the talking stage?

CHAPTER 5
SPRING, 1934

March 1, St. David's Day, 1934, I participated in the ritual songs and pageants to build us youngsters' pride in Wales. I played a leek, not being delicate enough to play a daffodil, but it was better than being a horse in Boadicea's chariot. Afterwards we had a half-day holiday.

Our gang's current favourite play-place was the sawmill. There the boxes for the tin and stamping-works were made. It was behind the railway station at one end of Glascoed Road, a row of tall, narrow, beige brick back-to-backs, some forty houses long. The entrance of the Rustbrook Tin Works was at the other end.

We were happier than pigs in mire playing in those sawdust dunes. They were as much fun as Barry Island sands. For burrowing and bouncing on, they almost beat a hayrick. You had to watch the fine, flying dust, not to get it in your eyes. The blustery March winds would kick it up in treacherous whirls. And our mongrel terrier, Nip the Second, would fling it in your face when he got a ferret-frenzy on. It was tickly to the nose, too. A peculiar sneezy smell. Mutilated wood, bruised cellulose.

That afternoon, above the whee-whee of the saws and planes, Bryn Thomas shouted suddenly, "Hey, look there, Vid."

I blew a pigtail shaving off my nose. "What, where?"

"Over by the works, coming out the gate."

A group of men in working clothes, swinging jacks and cans, crunched their steel-tipped boots along the dirt-and-pebbled back lane of Glascoed Road. What was surprising, my father strode along with them. He almost never took the main gate home, usually scwtching between the rusting fence wires to cross the railway line. That shortcut lopped a good five minutes off his homeward walk. It also by-passed the village pubs – a distinct advantage considering his taste for beer and his low threshold for temptation.

"What the hell did he come by *this* way for?" I said, trying to beat the sawdust off my green-striped pullover.

"To pick his pay up at the office window, p'raps?"

"But it ent pay-day, mun." To pay for coal next day, my mother had been searching pockets for loose cash.

We saw the group stop at a back-garden gate in the middle of the row of houses. They started to file through.

Bryn said, "Whose house is that?"

"Where Emrys Strong and his Mam live, I believe."

Now there was an even bigger puzzle. Although Emrys Strong was my father's age, he was nowhere in my father's orbit. He had some counting job which might have distanced him from the shift workers, but for his rabid politics. Emrys was tied to his mother's pinafore strings with a double reef knot, which didn't stop them fighting like cat and dog. He threatened during every spat to up and leave.

"Though damn slight odds he ever will," my father said. "Him and his old lady *relish* flying at each other's throats."

Emrys was at odds with everybody else as well. Nwd Probert's wife, reared opposite, contended that the trouble was, "Old Lady Strong be false as plates. Coddled him she *may* have, because of his clubfoot and shrunken arm. But deep down she was always secretly ashamed of him." This somehow had afflicted Emrys with incurable contrariness. He loved rebellious causes. He was always carping, always smoothing other people's fur against its natural grain. The only reason that my father and his mates would be going into *his* backyard would be for its convenience.

"What's up, I wonder, Vid?" said Bryn.

"Hell, don't ask me." I climbed up on a stack of boards to double my four foot ten. "I think they're going in the shed. Come on. Let's go'n have a quiz." If something was going on I wanted to know about it. To keep my father safe, as much as anything.

A little hole and platform landing-board under the eave of the shed's tar-papered roof, and a mess of blue-grey feathers and bird droppings confirmed my guess about whose house it was. Emrys was a pigeon-fancier. He was a familiar figure riding through the village on his push bike with the built-up pedal, a hamper full of homers strapped behind, going to compete or put them through a practice flight. His name was often in the *Argus* as trophy winner of some pigeon club.

Pigeon-fancying was second only to breeding and racing slinky, skinny greyhounds and whippets in our neighbourhood. Both were poor man's substitutes for horseracing at Ascot and regattas on the Thames. But Emrys didn't seem the sporty, outdoor type. For pastime, you'd have thought he would prefer to read or argue around the pubs. It wasn't till I was much older, after I knew more what he would and would not do, that it occurred to me to wonder at this incongruity. And to ask myself if the metal capsules on his carriers' legs mightn't have had more to do with his radical persuasion than with love of competition and the open air.

Bryn knit his hands to give me a leg-up on to the top of the brick wall. It formed a narrow ledge half way up the back of the shed.

I got a good grip on a corner upright. Bryn found a toehold in a crevice where mortar had crumbled from between the bricks, and I yanked him after me. We hugged the splintering planks and breathed in stifling fumes of creosote from the brittle roof. "Watch that bird pwp, mun," Bryn whispered as I fidgeted in place. My cheek was barely an inch clear of a wet half-crown blob of it.

I squinted through a knothole in the rough hewn boards.

"What can you see?" Bryn whispered.

"Not bloody much. A blasted pigeon's in the way." It was strutting back and forth across the hole, bowing and scraping and gobble-bobbling to its heart's content. "The bloody grit-box or the bath pan is blocking me on this side. Cwpy down and take a peep through that other crack."

He shuffled into position. "All I can see is your Dad sitting on a wicker basket next to Emrys Strong."

The pigeon moved clear of the chink. Though the field was narrow, by craning and gyrating, I made out Ruby Jones's father, Mr. Chesterton and Obie Dixon. They sat around on hampers and on sacks of maize and feed stacked against the wire-netting "windowed" wall. "They all look mean as sin and tamping mad," I said. "I back there's trouble at the works."

"I back there is," said Bryn.

It looked as though they were settling in for a long siege. To relieve our complaining muscles we slewed around and squatted on the ledge, dangling our feet.

Emrys Strong's voice said, "Have you had a bloody nuff, now, boyos? Are you ready to sign on with the CP?" Even if we couldn't see them, we could hear them well.

"Just about," Ted Swilling said. "This is the bloody end. I am full up to here."

Said Idris, "They do treat us like a pack of flaming dogs."

Uncle Jack, who assumed that volume made up for his snuffling impediment, roared, "More like a team of ruddy dray horses, if you ask me."

"Naih, mun. Not dogs nor horses, even," said my father. "They treat us like machines."

When the rumbling of assent subsided, Perce Cook said, "Will the Union back us to a strike, Obe?"

"Union be buggered," Bryn Thomas's father sneered. "It

was them steel chaps who are running it who got us *into* this predicament. T'ent no union of ours. It is a mockery."

"What's to stop us calling our own strike?"

"Defy the rotten lot by going slow at least."

Then Obie took the floor. "Hang on a minute, mates," he said and the hub-bub stopped. He was respected for the head he had between his shoulders. It was the reason they had chosen him shop steward. He had studied history and economics at Workers' Education night school, even algebra and literature. It was not unusual to see him working out equations on a steel bar with a bit of chalk. "Sweet is revenge," he went on evenly. "Lovely to go slow or strike. Nice to bring the owners to their knees, aye, aye. But what if it should break them, and the works close down for good?"

Only the cooing of the pigeons filled the silence.

"We are in a funny situation," he continued. "Between the devil and the deep blue sea. The tariff kicked the little independent tin works up the bott. The management are in a squeeze. All they can do is put the speed-up screws on us poor dabs. They can't afford to modernize."

Emrys tried to interrupt. The others squelched him with, "Pipe down, mun," and "Hush up a minute."

Obie went on, "What I'm saying is the steel-cum-tin-plate giants would *like* to see us strike. Play right into their hands. Why do you think Richard Thomas & Company connived to get the tariff? To eliminate us little outfits. Striking would be biting off our nose to spite our face."

The reedy voice of Austen Bishop piped, "You mean there ent much we can do about it, then?"

Emrys blew his cork. "I never thought I'd live to see my butties sympathize with bloody capitalists. Obie Dixon, you're no better than that renegade MacDonald." His voice was harshly mocking, working up to soapbox force. "Well, let me tell you something, mates. Nothing that you do, not even acting like a bunch of doormats, is going to stave off the evil day. Sooner or later those monsters will put paid to Rustbook. Buy it up dirt cheap and close it down."

A flick of fear crossed my heart, never to be completely quelled. It sparked a smoldering anger which gave me energy to try to understand these different ideas.

Perce Cook said, "What, then's, the good of anything?"

"There's one solution if you got the guts, mates," Emrys trumpeted. "Commandeer the works to run it for ourselves. Operate her as a workers' syndicate."

Loud silence met this foreign thought.

Emrys rattled on with his pet arguments. "If the people are too stupid to elect a government with guts enough to take over the means of production, we shall have to damn well seize the economic power piecemeal for ourselves."

"Capture the bloody works?" Tich Veasey's father screeched.

"God Almighty. There's ridiculous," my father rasped.

"They'd nab us in a minute, mun," said Uncle Jack, "and put us all in jug."

"Even assuming we could get away with it, there's not a bloody one of us knows how to run the place from A to Z."

Mr. Chesterton pleaded, "Come on, now, let's talk serious."

There was nothing more from Emrys. From the sound effects, he must have slapped his good right arm against his thigh and gone outside. It was like him to wash his hands of the whole business when he couldn't get his way.

Said Obie wretchedly, "I don't know any local action we could take that wouldn't pitch us from the pan into the fire. The change must come up top in government."

A chorus of sardonic laughs scoffed, not at Obie's view but at the likelihood of that ever happening.

"There must be *something*," Ruby Jones's father said, no doubt whittling his bit of wood as usual.

Idris said, "We could take a page out of the colliers' book."

"Them hunger marches to 10 Downing Street, you mean. And rallies in Trafalgar Square? Naih, mun. What good have *they* done? People don't have any sympathy no more."

Suddenly my father cried, "Jerusalem! Talking of *sympathy,* I know where there's some of that, by God."

As one voice, half a dozen butties chimed, "The Prince of Wales," and everybody laughed.

My father said good-naturedly, "Laugh all you want to, boyos, but *there* is a man with sympathy, by damn. In his heart he's asking the same questions we are: Why can't the government put every man jack of us to work? They have got to pay the dole, they might as well provide us jobs. Such as building roads and hospitals and schools. And houses, too. *There's* something he has shown a lot of interest in: decent housing for the common man. Maybe he's only waiting for a sign to rise and lead."

You would have thought the David we were celebrating as our Patron Saint that day was not some devout sixth-century monk but the Prince of Wales.

Perce Cook said, "Do you mean protest to him?"

"What Idris just suggested," my father said. "A hunger march."

Emrys must have come back in because we heard him roar, "Appeal to that yellow dog MacDonald? What a hope!"

"No, no," my father said. "Not to 10 Downing Street. To go and see the Prince. Right to his place in Windsor Castle Park."

Tense silence followed till Bryn Thomas's Dad said slowly, "It would be different."

Cautiously Ted Swilling said, "It ent at all a bad idea."

"I don't know how much good we'll do," Obie sounded cheerful, "but the news would pick it up as quite a stunt. Call attention to what's going on down here."

"Ooh, there's a bloody lark," Tich Veasey's father trolled.

The pigeons oog-oog-ooged and flapped their contribution to the happy pandemonium as my father's mumpy finally caught on.

So great was the need for action to discharge frustration, the March-on-Windsor idea spread like wild fire in a summer drought along the hill tops, through gorse and broom and bracken, dry as tinder, greedy for the spark.

By time the pubs and clubs closed that same evening, it had traveled clear along the Eastern Valley, top to bottom, up one side and down the other. My father knocked his staggered head to see the blaze he'd lit.

All the way up to Blaenavon went the word. There, disillusioned human relics of a once-thriving town had found out tariffs were no boon for them. Vague promises for reopening steelworks at the heads of valleys (abandoned for the seaboard when the industry switched to imported ores) had turned out to be lies. The town remained a place of ghosts and ashes. It was desperate for any action that might rekindle hope.

Even the tin-plate workers of Partridge, Jones & Patton, Pontypool, who made their own steel bar in Pontymister, responded heartily. Economic theory notwithstanding, tariffs had done little to improve their lot. The reaction at P.J. & P.'s Steel Sheet and Galvanizing works in Pontnewynydd, and Baldwin's in Panteg, was similar: "Please count us in."

Down as far as Newport flew the news. Lysaghts and Whitehead's people caught the fever. Word leapt the mountains to the tin-plate workers in Abercarn and Abertillery. Back came the question: "Can the Western and Sirhowy valleys join you, too, and make this all of Monmouthshire?"

And not just steel and tin-plate men, but colliers wanted

in. They had more than just the name of being militant for
their own ends. They wholeheartedly backed anyone who
made a show of strength.

"Men will be boys," my mother said on hearing of the
project. She tossed her head, eyes rolling ceilingward in
satiric comment. She said again, "Men will be boys," pleased
with her wit. I knew exactly what she meant. I had already
noticed boys like to move in packs or gangs. They delight
in secret rituals: the rites, trappings, cryptic symbols, insignia
and fancy costumes, pledges, blood oaths, sworn vows, all
to tie them tightly to each other. They crave camaraderie in
droves, the fellowship of teams and crowds. Banded together
they are in their element.

There was, of course, more motivation than the herd
instinct, or the desire for troop excitement. The March-on-
Windsor appealed to every man who experienced or was
threatened with the degradation of no work. Down Pill in
Newport, the coal trimmers and dock workers, pinched by
the fall-off in the coal and tin-plate export trades, clamoured
to take part.

"Come one, come all," my father said. Besides being in
expansive form, he abhorred all manner of exclusion or
exclusiveness, whether the snobbish social cutting of the
worker by the toffs, the segregating influence of wealth, or
the economic black-list against union men. More the better
to make a powerful impact on the Prince and Nation through
the press. More the merrier for that long trek to the Great
Park Windsor, where, in a ponderous pile called Fort
Belvedere, the Prince had made his home those past few
years.

"It's really quite a place by all accounts," my father said.
Since settling down to domesticity, albeit still without a wife,
the Prince had found he had a flair for gardening, fixing up

the ugly old place. He had chopped down dank and dreary yews to let in the sunlight, planted herbaceous borders, transplanted shrubs, set terraces and rock gardens, and cut winding paths into the woods.

If any further proof of spiritual affinity between my father and the Prince was needed, this was it. For a more dedicated amateur gardener than my father couldn't be found in seven valleys, even seven shires. He took many prizes in the local flower shows. His idea of an outing was to take my mother on an Amateur Gardeners' Association bus trip to see a glorious blaze of rhododendrons on the grounds of some estate, or visit the gardens in a public park. So, "It will be worthwhile to tramp there just to see the place," he said. He sometimes made it sound as if that was the *only* purpose that the Royal-March-on-Windsor had.

The first decision my father faced, as automatic leader of the enterprise, was the date. The natural choice was Whitsun, a festival traditionally associated with parades, Sunday School processions, mass rallying, and picnic teas.

"Let's see. Whitsun falls on May the twentieth this year," he said, leafing through a Christmas calendar with a garish coach and horses scene. "By then the weather will be fair, the cold and damp of winter gone. The heat and dust of summer not yet come. Lovely for a nice cross-country hike." A poet with the *hwyl* upon him.

There was one snag. "Good God above!" my mother scolded him. "It is bad enough you grown men acting like a pack of five-year-olds without losing work to do it." She was dolleying the sheets and heaving them into the copper, so she wasn't in a very pliant mood. Billowing steam had turned her sausage curls to lanky ringlets fringed with perm-end frizz. Her face and neck were red-streaked like a cochinealed blancmange. And just as damp and wobbly.

"No reason to lose any work," my father soothed her. "We can do it in our four days off." Under the tin-plate industry's "intermittent employment" policy, the workers now enjoyed a "short week" of three days.

"You can't hoof all that way and back in four days flat. Not unless you want to wear your feet down to the uppers."

"I never thought of that." My father's spirits sagged like a sausage-casing with the meat squeezed out. He gave his cheeks and chin a dry wash, and his hair a finger-comb.

"Well, think about it now, my man. And take your dirty feet off my clean fender. I didn't rub my fingers raw for you to muck it up."

Dismayed, he said, "When else, however?"

"I don't *care* when else. Or if at all." A sentiment shared by all the other scornful, penny-pinched wives, as it turned out.

The only other possibility was "August week" when the works closed for a fortnight's payless "holiday". But my father knew the weather then might be unbearable. Besides, he feared that date was too far distant to keep enthusiasm strong.

At the mere hint of postponement, the bubble of elation started to deflate. I suspected he'd soon start to feel a fool. But in the nick of time an event occurred to save his face. The Government suddenly announced in April its intention of making a new study of the Depressed Areas.

"You see!" my father crowed. "Just the rumble of us organizing made them shift themselves. I bet a tanner that the Prince got wind of our March and made them get a bloody move on." Maybe he couldn't prove it, but there *had* to be some cause-effect connection. Chance seldom came that close to making sense.

Postponement of the March to August now seemed meant to be. The study would be winding up about that time. A dramatic show of strength would spotlight the report so the Government couldn't shelve it like the one drawn up in 1931.

But this turn in events unfortunately cut both ways. Those hordes who had begged to be included were now content to rest upon their oars. "To scare the government off their bums was what we aimed to do by marching, wasn't it?" they said. "All right then, now we've made them move, we've got to give them a chance."

Only my father's loyal core of butties stood fast on their plan. Even many of those were somewhat light on dedication, being motivated rather by a fancy for adventure and a good excuse to get away from home than any nobler sentiment. But the net effect was all the same. In the shape that it was first proposed, as a demonstration by employees of the Rustbrook Tin-plate Works, the Royal-March-to-Windsor was still on.

CHAPTER 6
SUMMER, 1934

Throughout the spring and early summer, plans rolled ahead. The men pored over maps, calculated distances and speeds, and decided on their route and schedule.

"Any company I lead," my father said, "is going to do credit to themselves and where they come from, and honour the Royal mission they are on." To get them into top condition required a regular routine of discipline.

The company met up the mountain fields to drill. Like soldiers down at Newport barracks, they tramp-tramp-tramped around the golf links, their heavy boots squashing shiveryshakers and baby curls of ferns, crushing and beheading daisies or the satiny yellow blooms of celandines and buttercups, and tearing ragged robins into ribbons.

Crouched behind the bushy fringe of Roper's Wood, kneeling on the thick, packed pad of leaves and alder wings (some already on the sprout), Bryn Thomas, Ruby Jones and I collapsed in stitches at the sight of those old buzzards wobbling on their wonky pins. "They look like us when we were nippers playing soldiers," Bryn remarked. All they lacked were three-cornered hats of newspaper and broom-sticks at the slant.

The reason only us three hid out in Roper's Wood to watch their antics was that our old gang split up that year. Bryn had passed the scholarship to the County Secondary School for Boys, and Ruby Jones and I to Ponty Girls. The others in the gang either hadn't passed or didn't try. They pulled away, regarding us as snobs and swots. Bryn and I were forced to count old Ruby in; there was nowhere else for her to go. Fortunately, she was too much like a dun, soft little mole to be any bother. A poor, scraggy creature, so timid a bang-bursting paper bag would scare her to a froth.

As they trained, the men sang lustily their old war favourites: "Long, long way to Tipperary", "Pack up your troubles", "There's a long, long trail awinding". They sounded like a gaggle of squawking geese on a badly oscillating wireless. Never remotely like an Eisteddfod–winning choir. Still, the rhythm and the martial spirit were all there.

If the Royal Marchers weren't parading, they were limbering up their rusty limbs, touching toes, knocking shoulder blades together, bending knees. Sometimes they met at the second lock on the canal to limber up their rasping larynxes. Nwd Probert put them through selected pot-pourris of marching songs and the soaring melodies of Wales's national airs, "Ash Grove" and "Sospan Fach" included.

And if they weren't rehearsing, they were hunting out their tarnished medals and Brassoing them up, washing and ironing greasy ribbons, and snipping off the fray. Or daubing on the Cherry Blossom boot polish, or tapping soles. Down on their uppers they might be, but as long as they could scrape together a couple of coppers for a piece of leather and some tacks, and could borrow a cobbler's last, you wouldn't catch them looking down at heel. "Shabby you can't help, by damn," my father said. "But there is no excuse for holes and rips while there's still pride. No shame in darns and patches, is it, our Mam?" In a jovial mood, he was pleased to find agreement with a harmless one of my mother's prize humbuggeries.

My father brought a bare three pounds a week home all that summer. Yet he was as happy as a lark. He said it was because the Royal-March-on-Windsor would make inroads on the valley's problems. Actually the bustle and his being in the limelight was what buoyed him most. He even took in his stride our Muriel's departure from the nest. Shortly after she left school, she went to take up service in Penarth to train to be a maid for room and board.

As June wore on, anticipation mounted. More and more the March assumed the aura of a pleasure jaunt. If hunger marching meant hoofing it to Windsor on an empty stomach, then, "Pot! Our kind of march is something else," my father said. Much as he admired Gandhi, he thought his fasting-unto-death stunts rather overdoing it. They smacked too much of the starvation marathons of sideshow freaks. "As providers, we owe it to our families to come back hale and healthy. It's our job to keep on earning the few crumbs we can. It will be ample demonstration just to *walk* that far. No need to starve ourselves."

He also specified, "Besides our grub, we need our sleep. And all the decencies. I will not have us looking like a bunch of sloven tramps and beggars. We'll do it properly, or not at all. I don't care how the colliers done it. That is their affair. I can't see what's to gain from looking like a mess of skeling-tons and fish-heads our Nip drags from the ashcan."

The Supply Committee compiled lists, calculated weights of bedrolls, blankets, camping supplies, and finally concluded, "It ent humanly possible to pack the lot of it across our backs."

"Aih, get away. We did it in the army."

"Never this much. What's the point of taking it to look our best if it wears us out to carry it?"

"Aye, there's a point. So pare it down. Cut out the frills. To hell with extra socks."

The Supply Committee did its level best but, "We need a little van or summat bringing up the rear."

"It would violate the spirit of the March," my father said.

"Not if it's a Red Cross Ambulance. If someone wrenched his ankle or got heat prostration, we couldn't leave them lying by the road."

"True." My father had a sudden thought. "Half a bleeding tick. I think I know the very thing."

I knew what he was going to say. His well-worn quip, "Our Maker did assign us the same wavelength," contained more truth than jest.

The previous week my mother had complained that the middle kitchen chimney wasn't drawing as it should. A spell of summery weather had saved her lighting fires there for several weeks. When at last she did, the chimney smoked. "Especially when the wind whips from the east, Fred, or when the passage door is open."

My father set fire to the chimney to burn out the soot. I went outside to watch the multi-coloured flames leaping from the chimney pot. Sparks cascaded down the roof. "Dear God, he'll have the house on fire," my mother cried. "They can see it from the police station. Old Russell will be up to caution us."

My father poked his head out of the window, and she reprimanded him, "Dull fool!"

To which he forcefully rejoined. "Dear Christ, you wanted me to do it. You are too mingy to put out the money for a sweep."

When the flames died down and we went inside, relief turned to dismay. Soot filled the grate and hearth and smudged the mat. My father stood there in the middle of it looking, by his own description, "like a shwtten golliwog".

Sounding sick, my mother chided, "Oh, Fred."

"*I* didn't do it, mun," he whined. "T'was that." He nudged a black lump just inside the fender with his toe.

My mother peered at it. "What in the world –?"

"Dead bird. The buggers must have built a nest up there and clogged it up."

After all the fuss and mess, the fire still didn't draw. Soot fell in dibs and dabs. To my mother's chagrin, we had to have the sweep come after all.

Our choice was Barney O'Quirk, our rag-and-bone man. He brought his horse and cart to our street every month or so. When I heard him clack his clappers and shout, "Any rags, bottles and bones?" I would dash into the coalhouse for the little pile of junk I had collected. Then I'd rush out to the cart to get the couple of ha'pence Barney calculated it was worth.

There weren't too many rags and bones to collect in those hard-up times. Sunday joints were small and dogs were hungry. The hand-me-downs were handed down and down again, made over till they fell to pieces, then put to use as dusters, dishrags, floor cloths, or stuffing for a cushion or a toy. Barney had to supplement his income with various odd jobs on the side. He hauled coke from the gasworks in the shadow of whose frightening gasometer he lived, sold flashing stick in bundles house to house, and swept chimneys at a cut-rate price. He did anything a horse and cart was useful for.

Barney was a puny, stunted runt from generations of his forebears working in the darkness of the pits with potatoes as their staple fare. He would have been an ideal size for crawling up the cavernous chimney of a mansion – if he only counted mansion-occupants among his clientele.

Slight, with a crumpled face and large, high-pricking ears, he looked as Irish as an Irish *pwca*. Born and bred down in The Hammer, he was, however, as much a native son of Gwent as my father or myself. "Yet than Erin," Barney claimed, "there is no dearer place on earth."

That sentiment was all the more peculiar when you remembered Barney's father was also born and bred in Monmouthshire.

In fact, it was doubtful any O'Quirk had trodden the hallowed soil since Barney's great-grandfather was herded into Wales by the joint force of potato famine and the English ironmasters a century before. The fact that those Irish immigrants were treated worse than cattle no doubt stimulated them to cherish a double dream of paradise: earthly and celestial.

My mother made a point of having Barney only while my father was at home. "He's Irish, isn't he?" was all she'd say. Originally, the native Welsh had all the craftsmen's and the foremen's jobs in the iron workings and the collieries. The foreign Irish served as common labourers, hauling limestone, slag and coal. The Welsh kept their distance from the Irish also on religious grounds. The Welsh were righteous Nonconformists, whereas the Irish foundered in the vulgar sensualities of popery: worshipped graven images, drank, danced, played cards and used foul language. And look at how the kids kept coming.

The Welsh and Irish being Celtic cousins, and both being put on by the exploiting English ever since marauding Anglo-Saxons first set foot on British soil, a lot more should have joined them than divided them, was the way my father looked at it. "The powerful do always flourish on the petty bickerings and jockeyings of fools," he said. "Will we ever learn?"

People like my father helped soothe the intertribal rancour between the Paddies and the Taffies. Economic levelling and even fraternizing had begun. Barney repaid my father's genuine fondness by fetching him a load of dung or leaf mould gratis, or a bag of bone meal or some lime at bargain price. My father gave him bedding-out plants in exchange, or a nice bouquet of white chrysanths to deck the altar now and then.

That particular day, while he stretched his tarp across the hearth, Barney happened to remark, "How are you coming on with the Royal March then, Fred?"

"Going along beautiful."

"Marvelous idea of yourn." Barney jointed pieces of long handle on to his round, flat brush. "But better the way you had it first going off, when you'd let anybody join."

"We let anybody join right now as wants to, Barn. Them as dropped out, dropped out of their own accord."

"Naih! You mean *anybody* is still welcome in?"

My father's genuine broadmindedness blinded him not only to prejudice, but sometimes to the sensitivities of victims of prejudice. He didn't catch on that Barney was angling for special reassurance that a non-tin-working, slum-dwelling, Irish rag-and-bone man would be wholeheartedly received.

To tip my father off, I piped, "Why aren't you going with them, Barney?"

He hung his head. "Oh, I don't know."

My father's penny dropped. "Law sakes, aye, aye. Why don't you, mun? You would be a credit to us, Barn. We don't have any shopkeepers or anyone in business on his own account. You would very nicely represent that end of it. You are hurt by bad times just as much as us."

Barney's face lit up like a carved turnip head on Roasting Guyer-Hallowe'en.

My father said, "I'd have made a special point to ask you sooner, mun, if I'da known. But I thought the reason that you didn't volunteer was you not being very partial to the British royalty. Back when the Irish Republican Army was kicking up you were all against the British Crown."

"Aye, but the Prince ent like the scum who plagued the Irish all these years before we got Home Rule. He is for the underdog. Even an untouchable in India ent beneath his sympathy. I am underdog and down-and-out, so I'm for him."

There was just one problem. Barney had never left Mavourneen overnight. He and his aged Welsh pony were inseparables. He'd have to feel his way and find out if she'd stand the break. Even if she looked like being brave, who would board her lovingly while he was gone? His missus was long dead, his considerable brood grown up and flown the coop.

"So that is how we'll solve this knotty problem, mates," my father cheered the Supply Committee. "Kill half a dozen bloody birds in one fell swoop: carry a week's rations, have an ambulance, and let old Barney have his cake and eat it, too."

The conflict had been wrecking Barney. He was overjoyed to hear the news. He planned to give the cart a coat of bright green paint topped by the regulation blood-red crosses on a white field as per the conventions. He also planned to garland paper shamrocks on Mavourneen's harness, and plait crepe paper streamers down her tail.

Emrys poured cold water on the campaign from the start, of course. "What in the name of Christ do you hope to gain? Except callouses and bunions, blisters and stiff knees."

It was sour grapes. His dream of glory had always been to lead a mass revolt. Although the March fell a long way short of that, he would have given his sound arm to have fitted in my father's boots.

When he heard that Barney's horse and cart were going, he didn't miss his chance to snipe. He gave a good performance of a laughing fit. "If you had only *told* me," he sputtered between chortles, dabbing his eyes, "I'd have gone up on the turnpike and talked one of them gypsy chaps into loaning you his bloody caravan."

The gypsies Emrys had in mind were not the kind that swing tambourines and singsongs of Romany around their camp fire. The characters that we called gypsies shared the general poverty, and were a far cry from the ones you read about in books. You could conjure up a gaudy, ramshackle old caravan, pots and pans swinging from its sides, bumping and creaking, behind the Royal March. A grubby, hard-eyed gypsy would be sitting on the wagon-front geeing-up his mangy horse while his ragged half-starved woman walked alongside, ready to start peddling pegs from the basket on her arm, the kids straggling behind.

I hid my face by furiously continuing to weed the onion and lettuce beds.

Emrys rubbed in salt. "I reckon you'll be hiring a bloody brass band next."

As a matter of fact, my father had given that some thought. Ideally, he would have liked a military band in regimental uniform, the drummer beating out a martial "Men of Harlech" pace. As second best, he had sounded out the conductor of the Pontbran Fireman's Band. Lester Croaker was a white-collar worker in a Newport factory. He would scarcely have lowered himself to associate with a pack of crude old working men with radical proclivities. With hypocritical excuses, he had turned my father down.

Emrys baited, "Harry Winters would oblige you with the Salvation Army Band, I bet. Do your souls a lot of good to sing hymns all that way and back. Or how about that character band from up the Rhondda? You know, the one that won the Royal Gwent Carnival's top prize last year. With all those orange and purple costumes. And the tassels and gold braid." But then, "Oh, damn, you can't get *them*. They'll be competing in the Carnival, no doubt, the week you plan to leave."

When Emrys limped away, still sneering, my father said,

"Poor bugger. That's his nature, to pee on blazes. Deep down he's really grieved he can't come with us with his gammy leg."

"We could carry him along in Barney's cart," suggested Idris. But nobody would dare broach Emrys with the offer. He would have scorched the hair clean off the head of anyone who showed awareness of, let alone compassion for, his disability.

Later, Emrys's needling went nearer the bone. "You know the toffs go out of London in the summer, don't you, mates? After traipsing all that way you won't find anybody home. There's a lot of bloody idiots you'll look."

Obie told my father privately, "He may not be far wrong, Fred. The Prince is always off on jaunts to some place in the Empire." So they wrote to Mr. Arthur Jenkins, Labour MP for our constituency, and also to the Secretary of the TUC. The first reply said, "Regret to inform you the calendar of His Royal Highness schedules a visit to the South of France the entire month of August." And his calendar was filled up beyond Christmas.

"Well there it is," my father said, his emotions enormously compressed. But the muscles around his mouth worked overtime and his eyelids trembled.

To save him breaking down and losing face in front of Obie, I said, "It's only a postponement. There'll be another chance."

"Can't do it in the winter," my father said.

I said, "Next spring I meant."

I guessed he was thinking it would be hard to hold the group together. Still, his mumpy would take care of that. It was as inveterate as Tich Veasey's peeping-Tom compulsion, though of vastly higher rank. I might smile at it behind my hand, but it was a magnificent obsession for all that, with the noblest of motives: justice for the common man.

As a consolation prize, the contingent took part in the Royal Gwent Carnival parade on an early-closing afternoon of August week. They got some fine rounds of applause from the crowds who lined the Newport streets. But for my father it was still only second best.

CHAPTER 7
AUTUMN, 1934 TO SPRING, 1935

Two promising developments helped ease their disappointment at the cancellation of the March. First, there was talk that the Prince would visit Wales in connection with King George's Silver Jubilee the following spring. They would keep their corps in readiness for that heart-quickening event.

The second was the growing hope that the government's renewed concern for the area, as reflected in the on-going study, would bear sound fruit.

Not until November were the investigators' shocking findings forced into the open. There were widespread reactions of dismay and fear. The facts were these: Sir Wyndham Portal found almost fifty percent unemployment in South Wales. Three quarters of the unemployed had had no regular work for a year or more; more than one fifth had had none for five. In derelict ghost towns at the heads of valleys more than two-thirds had been idle many years.

The iron and steel and galvanized sheet workers with forty percent unemployment were almost as badly off as the colliers with forty-five. In the tin-plate industry about a third were out of work.

None of this was news to the South Wales workers. They had experienced first hand the suffering those cold figures failed to tell. What came as a startling blow was the report's conclusion that not more than half those currently on unemployment rolls could hope for "reabsorption" into local industry. The rest were "permanent surplus" unless some fast and drastic moves were made.

The Government so got the wind-up that they immediately

appointed commissioners to develop programmes for revival of the areas. Mr. Malcolm Stewart was chosen for South Wales. And on November 26 1934, the Depressed Areas (Development and Improvement) Bill was introduced in Parliament.

There was a great fanfare during the debates in Commons to suggest some big, bold action in the offing. Not being barristers or solicitors, my father and his butties took on trust remarks like those of Mr. Neville Chamberlain, then Chancellor of the Exchequer, of what the bill would do, "What we want here . . . is something more rapid, more direct, less orthodox . . . than the ordinary plan. We have resolved to cut through all the ordinary methods . . . We are going to give the Commissioners a very wide discretion. They must not be afraid of trying experiments."

At the last minute in the bill's progress through the House of Lords, they crossed out the word "depressed" and put "special" in its place, as if removal of the stigma of the word would remove the embarrassing facts themselves.

"Typical bourgeois gentility!" sneered Emrys. "No guts to face the brutal facts of life. That should tip you off what good this bloody bill will do."

In subsequent months the government got wrapped up in the upcoming celebrations of the Silver Jubilee. The official reason given for the size of the to-do was that the nation craved to express its deep affection for Their Majesties. My father wouldn't swallow that. "I vow the biggest reason for the fuss is that scab MacDonald's taste for sucking up to all the nobs. The fawning lickarse enjoys tripping back and fro to Court every whipstitch, got up in them fancy dresses. A frock coat or them silly knickers." My father didn't go as far as Emrys Strong, who contended royal ceremony no less than religion was the opiate of the masses. But he did hold that the British public was "like a lot of bloody kids looking for any old excuse to break up the monotony." With their pathetic appetite for glamour, the women were the worst. Witness the effect the "fairy-tale" marriage of the Duke of Kent and the Greek Princess Marina had had on them and on their clothes the previous November.

"You miserable killjoy!" crabbed my mother. "The poor old King and Queen deserve their due."

"Oh, I don't begrudge the old sods some palaver, mun," my father said. "For all he said he wouldn't lower hisself to invite a Labour man inside his palace, old George has been a good king as kings go. By and large he has kept his snooty nose out of where it don't belong. But it is just that I am like that son of his. Don't hold with wasting precious time and money on frivolousness when there are people suffering."

The projected visit of that royal son to his Principality was soon confirmed. He would appear in Cardiff the Saturday following the Jubilee. The Royal Marchers took satisfaction not only in the shorter journey (no loss of work), but the fact His Royal Highness would see the region's problems with his own two eyes. The corps resumed intensive drilling.

The Prince's scheduled visit made it easier for my father to put up with all the rigmarole. Without the celebrations, there would be no glorious side benefit of his idol's flesh-and-blood appearance. It put him in a mellow mood to think his mumpy had a chance to be fulfilled. Beside, he was no spoilsport. The way he looked at it, "You don't have to believe in witches, do you, to enjoy the fun of Roasting Guyer-Hallowe'en."

We all threw ourselves wholeheartedly into the gala preparations. Yards of red, white and blue crepe paper were braided into "chitterlings" – they must have made a million tons of it that year. We festooned these decorations around the windows, from house to house, and back and forth across the street.

My mother played the old out-besting game. She blew her corset fund, saved up in a bluebird toffee box, on giant flags. Determined to stay top when she was copy-catted, she had my father pot a dozen primulas to decorate the windowsill. And all along the street, out came the pots of ferns and aspidistras, dusty everlasting flowers and pampas grass, jam jars of catkins, pussy willows, bluebells, violets and primroses from Roper's Wood. Bossy old Meg Morgan displayed her commemorative mug collection going back to Queen Victoria's Golden and Diamond Jubilees.

The Day was gloriously balmy. Makeshift trestle tables set up in the street were laden with cherry-splotched Genoa cake, loaf cake, plain and seed cake and all kinds of sand-wiches. Heavy bowls of trifle and blancmange, in patriotic colours and motifs, anchored damask tablecloths.

After we dispatched the party fare, the whole village went over to the recreation field beside the park to take part in the sports and races. In the women's egg-and-spoon event, my mother waddled down the turf, her china egg balanced on her wooden ladle almost to the finish tape. To watch her plunge arse-over-tip and show her bloomers and garters was the best laugh of the day.

My father won a beaker in the sack race with his cunning little bunny-hop technique.

The Lanzos did a roaring trade. There was one Italian family in almost every village in our region, running the sole cafe. Ours were the Lanzos. Though they held them-selves aloof, they were a part of us. The boys, our generation, were respected for the hard work they put into their business, and the way they looked after their mother when their father died.

Their pony Annabella, who drew their hokey-pokey cart, was all got up in leghorn hat trimmed with poppies, daisies and delphiniums. The wagon was wheel-deep in kids buzzing like wasps around a jar of bramble jam. Ben Lanzo would have been in my class if they hadn't sent him to the Catholic School. His job was to scoop ice cream into ha'penny cornets. Vincent slapped penn'orths between wafer biscuits in his oblong metal mould. Salvatore, the eldest, raked in the cash beside the cart.

"Hi, Ben," I called. With any luck, my claim upon his friendship would help me jump the queue as I got close. "How you been, mun? How is tricks?"

"Bloody busy, mun," he muttered. "You're lucky you can play on holidays."

As I elbowed close I noticed that a table charged with pop and jars of pink and yellow sherbet flanked the far side of the cart. It was superintended by a tall, young fellow who bore a marked resemblance to the Lanzos in a handsome, flashy way. His large eyes glinted like lumps of high grade coal. His hair sheened bluely like a well-fed blackbird. He cut a very striking figure dressed in black from head to toe.

As Salvatore fumbled for my ha'penny change in the leather pouch slung from his shoulder, I asked him, "Who is that, then, over there?"

"Him? He's my cousin Angelo."

Nonchalantly licking ice cream, I sauntered past the table to study Angelo. He seemed excessively agreeable, especially to the older girls, a lot of whom appeared to have a powerful thirst. The pop they bought from him was not the stuff in bottles. It was the cheaper stuff he mixed from sherbet in a large enamel jug. I knew from long experience that sherbet was the right strength when diluted by one's spit alone. The brew he concocted must have tasted only slightly less watery than water itself. Yet the giggling girls were buying it as though it were the nectar of the gods. He had the gall to call it "homemade lemonade". He was cagier than a London barrow boy.

When I was down to the last crunchy nibble of my cornet, a lull occurred in Angelo's trade. He began stacking boxes.

I wiped my sticky fingers on my knickers and went to help him heave a case of fulls.

"Thanks, love." He grinned and cocked his head as though to ask me why and who.

"I'm a friend of Ben's," I said. "Viddy Williams. Sal told me you're his cousin Angelo."

"That's right. I am much obliged."

His English sounded fluent, but the rhythm of his speech was different from the singsong of the Welsh or the English la-di-da. "Where you come from? Italy?"

"I've been here about two years."

"So where you been till now?"

"London." He scooped some raspberry sherbet for a tot into a square, penny bag.

"What doing?"

"Factory in Paddington. Loading biscuits in big boxes on to lorries."

"You drive?"

"A bit I do, sometimes. When a regular driver is off sick."

"There's lucky," I said. "That is my ambition when I'm old enough."

He laughed. "But you're a girl!"

"What odds?" I said indignantly. "I got hands and legs like you."

He started shifting the empties around to make more room. Again I lent a hand. "Why have you come down here, then, mun?"

"No work." He apparently didn't mind my being inquisitive. "I lost my job."

"Why's that?"

"Bit of bad blood. Anyway, us foreigners are always first to go and last to get put on again."

"There ent no work down here, though, neither. Our Dad says it is worse than London."

"So I gather. But these are my only relatives in England. My sponsors as they say. It is their duty to look after me if I'm hard up."

Except on gala days like these, the Lanzos made a very shaky living from their café in the village. And there were quite a crew of Lanzo mouths to feed. As if he read my thoughts, he said, "If the situation don't improve, I'll go back home. The army's crying out for chaps like me. There is going to be one hell of a big blow-up before long."

I had been reading something in the paper about Italian claims on Abyssinia, and guessed that he was talking about that. "You're going to grab the desert from the natives, is it?"

Angelo said haughtily, "Italy will take what rightfully belongs to her. She won't put up with interference from the League in Ethiopia." He said it in a patly pompous fashion like the Reverend Willie Spinum quoting Bible verses. His eyes' bright glint and his curled lip warned me I shouldn't get involved.

I broke the tension by requesting a ha'pennyworth of sherbet. My estimation of him swung again when, smiling, he pushed my paying hand away. "I'll give you some for helping me," he said.

Some bigger girls arrived to buy his ditch water. I retreated to enjoy my spoils. I laid the tangy particles across my tongue with a moistened index finger. It was soon dyed crimson to the second knuckle. Trickles stained my hand. I felt six again.

Just then our Muriel approached the table where Angelo dispensed his pop and charm. She had been given the entire week off from her job. Her employers had gone up to London for the celebrations. They had kindly given her her annual payless holiday to coincide with their own vacation period.

The year had made a change. She had left a gawky girl in plaits and come back bobbed and all filled out. Even I couldn't help admitting she looked fetching in the "jubilee" dress my mother had made for her as a surprise. A silky white thing trimmed with red and blue. A flared skirt and a tight red belt to emphasize her tiny waist. Two rows of tri-coloured bull's-eye buttons closed the bodice opening, the second row being compliments of me. They had been intended for my blouse, but I had spurned them as ridiculous.

Being blonde and fragile, our Muriel contrasted vividly with Angelo. I frowned to see her simper at the come-into-my-parlour gleam in his dark eyes.

As innocent as daisies in the spring, I sidled up to her, "Hello, our Mu."

"What are you doing here?" She was startled and annoyed.

Smiling enigmatically between us, Angelo inquired of me, "Is this your sister?"

"Aye."

"Please present me, then."

I mumble-fumbled my way through the introductions, and Angelo repeated, "Mu?" His voice caressed the name, his eyes the named.

"Short for Muriel," she said. A lovely pink washed over her pale face. Their hands touched as she took a glass of pop from him. Her eyes turned indigo. Her swooping lashes fluttered. Like people kissing in the pictures, the whole business revolted me.

I saw no more of them until the evening. My mother came looking for me shortly afterwards. She wanted me to go and keep tabs on my father – he had disappeared.

He was purportedly rehearsing with the corps of Royal Marchers for the Saturday excursion. But when I found him they were actually in the Two Locks pub. They were in high spirits, toasting the Prince instead of his old man. If you'd lit a match, the whole place would have gone up in a fireball.

When I got my parents back together, the evening festivities were just beginning. It was nearly time to light the bonfire beacons along the mountaintops. The fireworks were soon to start. Displays of Union Jack and Crown & Sceptre had been promised on the Clarkeville rise.

My father said, "Where is our Mu to, Vid?"

"I saw her just a bit ago."

My mother said, "Who with?"

"I didn't notice. Gwyneth Price, I 'spect."

"I'll go and find her." My father started to take off.

In a rare coincidence of views, my mother and I said "No" together. *I* should be the one to go.

Seconds after leaving them, I accosted Gwyneth Price. "It is no good acting dense," I told her when she made a play of ignorance. "I know who she is with." But she only laughed.

I saw Eunice Roberts at the dancing in the street down by the Cenotaph. She hee-hawed when I asked her if she'd seen our Muriel. "I thought you were her pal!" I said, disgusted.

I cross-examined everyone I knew, a good half of the people there. Drawing attention to the fact that she wasn't in the public safety zone could not have done her reputation any good. "Off up the canal, spooning, brazen little madam, I expect," said Esther Jarrett.

From Beak the Meat, "If she was mine a good smack bottom she would get."

That was the angle that I worked on next. The canal bank was a lovers' lane. By now, three parts anxiety, two parts curiosity and only one obedience drove me on. I had to hurry. Dusk would thicken into darkness soon.

On the far side of the sports field a track led up a brambled slope. I aimed for that. The field was empty now, though the strings that had marked the parallel courses for the heats still snared the ground. By time I'd picked my way across, scattered Roman Candles were alight, and Vesuviuses splashed the sky.

On a grassy flat beside the brook, I heard hushed voices. Approaching stealthily, I saw our Muriel and Angelo stretched out on the grass. By the kittenish way she snuggled up to him, I knew she was as hypnotised as a rabbit on its back.

I had always known she was a simpleton. She would trust the devil if his words were sweet. I had never visualized her in this sort of predicament, and was at a loss how to cope with it. All I had to go on were the crude stories and secret, garbled information picked up on the street. I knew instinctively, however, that the situation called for some finesse.

I had the benefit of two rows of buttons on my sister's dress, the second row thanks to my good sense. It gave me time to think. The best thing to do was try whistling nonchalantly like a casual passer-by. But my lips were stiff and wouldn't pucker.

Like a miracle sent to save me, a corker of a noise, like a salute of twenty-one guns fired altogether, split the sky. The prelude of the rockets saved the day.

Our Muriel squealed. Angelo jumped up, throwing his hands high as though a rifle had been emptied in his back. Our Muriel said hoarsely, "Blessed Lord. Our Dad will be out looking for me. I shall get the strap."

I ducked and dodged on the way back to the park, keeping them in sight. The signs suggested merely a postponement of that amorous interlude. I had a major problem on my hands.

To put a spoke in her wheel, I wrote a letter on brown paper in an alien backhand. "Dear Madam, You were seen last night carrying on with that Iti fellow. Your name will be dirt if you don't watch out."

I put it in the post with an uncancelled stamp steamed off

an envelope, and hoarded for this kind of an eventuality. I
marked it "Local" to make sure Arthur Hoare-the-Post would
drop it through our letterbox on the afternoon delivery. I
wanted to be there when the knocker rattled.

When she opened it, her face turned all the colours in the
puce-to-beetroot range. She kept popping into the front room
to re-read it.

After a bit she showed the envelope to me. "Do you know
this writing?"

I pursed my lips inspecting it. "It looks like the Reverend
Willie Spinum's. Why?"

"Oh, no," she croaked.

"It might," I said, "be Mr. Enoch Stokes, the Prims." He
was a Bible-thumping minister at the Primitive Methodists.

She was eyeing me now in a doubtful way. Perhaps I had
overdone it, making her suspicious. I said quickly, "But show
it to our Mam. She's ever so good at reading people's
writing." I looked up, even more sweetly helpful. "Didn't
the letter say who it was from?"

That had her bending over backwards to be nice to me.
She was terrified I'd let it out about the letter. It might pre-
cipitate a cross-examination by my mother that would hang
her by the end of it.

It was impossible to keep her always in my sights that
week she was at home, but I tended to believe her when she
told my mother she was only going out with Gwyneth Price
and company. Still, I was glad when she returned to work. I
doubted Angelo would pursue her to Penarth.

She left the following Saturday. That was the same day Lloyd
George had arranged to bring the Prince to Cardiff for the
Jubilee. So she had an escort of the Royal Marchers going
back by train. At the last minute they had decided that it
would be pointless to march the distance overnight. Everyone

would be in bed. There'd be no one to impress along the way.

But we got a dress rehearsal of their intended presentation to the Prince. They assembled at the Pontbran Cenotaph and paraded through the village, gathering a fair-size crowd to see them off. Dressed in their best pinstripe suits, copiously be-medalled, with bowler hats, their faces scrubbed, their hair trimmed, and their toe-caps sparkling, they did us proud.

It was the middle of the night when my father stumbled up the stairs. It was Sunday noon before he put in an appearance. If bleary, red-rimmed eyes and the pallor underneath his stubble was anything to go by, it must have been a real Red Letter Day.

"It wasn't like what we hoped for the Royal-March-on-Windsor," he answered my enquiry. "That was only what you would expect. Seeing that there were a lot more pebbles on the beach than us. Everybody and his missus from the valleys must have been there. Not to mention all their kids."

"So you didn't get to talk to him?"

He gave a wistful laugh as he wound the clock. "No, Vin, we didn't. A big festivity like that, you could see at once it was not the time or place. Gorstruth, you never seen such hordes. The place was packed. Our little muster wouldn't even have got a look-in, except old Barney found a half-a-dozen orange crates to stack against a wall. We stood on those and made a nice, neat line, snapping to attention and saluting as he passed. He flicked his hand halfway between returning our salute and waving, so we know he noticed us. Bless his dear old smiling chops, it did my heart good to set eyes on him. He is more popular than ever. Wales has reason to be proud of him."

But I doubted this brief sight would keep my father satisfied for long.

CHAPTER 8
SUMMER TO AUTUMN, 1935

All other things being equal, that glimpse of his Dear Idol would have held my father for a while. But shortly afterwards, Richard Thomas & Company announced that it intended shutting down some of its South Wales operations and moving them to Redbourn, Lincolnshire. The move was to "rationalize" the industry – to cut costs by erecting an integrated, streamlined, American-style strip mill on the Redbourn site. The way it was explained to me, the ore would go in one end and come out the other finished tin-plate. This was the largest steel-cum-tin-plate firm in Britain. It controlled a good two-fifths of all the tin-plate industry.

There was great outrage. They had promised jobs. Instead, they were draining the lifeblood out of us. The general economic blight had now come close to home. My father stood to lose his job. We'd have to live on the shabby payout of the dole. I realized I might have to leave school. I felt a huge surge of resentment, fear and anger. I wanted to do something, but had no idea what.

Emrys made hay of the situation. "You can't blame the company for not being concerned with the lives they ruin." Emrys loved to lay on the sarcasm with a trowel. "Their responsibility is to the stockholders to plumpen up the profits. It is progress, look."

He was no more bitter than my father. Anyone with a stake in South Wales was up in arms. Labour MPs, local authorities, related industries and other interested bodies made representations both to the company and Cabinet throughout the summer in an effort to ward off the dreadful blow. Tension mounted in the valleys and by summer's end everything was ready to go whoof with spontaneous combustion. Emrys and his comrades stood by to fan the spark.

When the authorities appeared to be getting nowhere, my father agonized, "Chrissakes, there must be *something* we can do." Something short of the violence that Emrys wanted to stir up. Something more in keeping with his democratic faith. Something that the rank and file themselves could execute – and fast. But nothing would suggest itself.

A few days later, his mumpy took a bright new turn. He was out in the back kitchen, his face daubed with lather, stropping his razor as though for use on Richard Thomas & Company's collective throat, when he suddenly said to the mirror, "Blow me! Why not *telephone* the man?"

He rushed out on the bailey, his face still swathed in foam, and yelled across the wall. Idris came out, waving a large meat bone he'd been picking for his tea.

My father cried, "I got it, Id. Why don't us try to reach him on the telephone?"

"Who's'at, Fred?" Idris said, slobbering flecks of meat.

"The Prince of Wales!"

Up the shed around the stove that evening, his other butties were no more impressed than Idris. Ted said, "They'd never put us through."

Bryn's father said, "Even if we got through to the Fort, some bloody butler'd answer it."

"Nothing bloody venture, nothing bloody gain, I always thought," my father flared. It made him seethe to have his brilliant suggestions always fall on barren ground.

"Don't it cost to telephone all that way, Fred?"

"Only a bob or two at most. Surely to God we can forego a couple of pints of booze or a packet of fags in a worthwhile cause." Without waiting for the others to react, he worked himself into a paddy of disgust. "But if you're all so bloody mean you can't chip in a threepenny bit, I'll pay the bloody lot myself." He hunted furiously in his pockets and slapped down a sixpence and a shilling and a couple of pennies, one by one. The fumbling threw his timing off and robbed the gesture of dramatic punch.

"It wasn't the money that was worrying me. Only who would do it," said Ted Swilling, as though that had been settled now. He felt round in his pockets, jingling change, and flamboyantly brought out half a crown. The others quickly followed suit, though not on such a generous scale. Their willing contributions backed up Ted's position that their previous reluctance wasn't due to lack of faith or stinginess.

What they feared was having to use the alien contraption of a telephone. There weren't more than a half a dozen instruments in our village at the time. It would have taken a pretty dire emergency to force any of my father's butties to use the public kiosk in the Post Office.

My father saw too late that he had built himself a trap. He quickly tried to extricate himself. "Obie'll do it, won't you, Obe?"

"Naih, mun. I wouldn't have the brass."

"To hell with all of you. A fine pickle we'd be in if we never tried."

Ted said, "Then you will do it, Fred?"

"Damnright, I will." But I knew how much he dreaded it.

The next few days were hell for him. The thought of tackling the baffling mechanics of the telephone gave him the cold sweats. He had never, to my knowledge, used one before. But that was the smallest of his worries. Far more awesome was the prospect of talking to the Prince. He spent long periods down the bailey in the lav or up the shed, composing and rehearsing. It was more troubling than amusing to hear him hullo-ing His Royal Highness – talking to himself.

In the end he wrote down on a piece of cardboard the things he planned to cover in the conversation. He invited me to go along. He needed me to hold the prompter up for him, of course. But I suspected I was needed just as much to keep him company and give him confidence. He didn't want any of his mates there to hear him make a jackass of himself. Whereas, if I should guffaw when he fluffed, though I might get my ears boxed for my impudence, he knew I'd never cop on him.

The first thing he did when we went into the post office was to change Ted's half crown into sixpences and coppers. While he was at the counter, I wished he would ask Mrs. Alsopp to show him how to use the phone. But he was too sensitive, his pride too great, to expose himself to ridicule from such as her.

We crammed into the kiosk like jelly babies in a jar, both as jittery as tadpoles.

Years later, when distance dimmed anxiety and shame and we could laugh about the incident, he reminisced, "Duw, Duw. There is a bag of nerves I was. And the muddle that I made of it."

"Remember pressing the wrong button, A for B, or B for A?"

"And letting drop my tuppence by mistake?"

"And the awful job you had persuading the GPO tele-phonist you weren't having her on? That you really did want her to connect you with Fort Belvedere?"

"And all the time that nosey bitch Blanche Alsopp craning out to watch us through the glass?"

When they finally put him through and he released his money, his face dripped with sweat. His cheeks flamed brighter than his usual furnace burn. He moved so wildly and erratically that when he nudged me to hold up the card, he poked an elbow in my eye. He nearly pushed me through the door when I put my ear close to the phone.

"Hello, hello," he burst out in a high, cracked voice. Then, in a swankier intonation as he had heard them say it on the wireless, "Are you there?"

He held the earpiece well away as though he feared it might bite his ear off. I heard a crackling, then a hollow midget voice said, "Who is calling, please?"

"Fred Williams," my father shouted. "Be this the Prince of Wales, your Royal Highness, if you please?"

There was a pause. The midget voice took on a haughty edge. "Please hold the line."

My father took the opportunity to lick his lips and mop his brow. He sighed a deep, "Oh, Christ," just as the receiver came alive again.

"Hello, may I help you?" the receiver said.

My father started violently. "Your Royal Highness?" His voice filled the kiosk and leaked outside. Blanche Alsopp's head bobbed into view.

The earpiece said, "I am His Royal Highness's personal secretary. I regret to say His Royal Highness is not presently available." The voice was cultivated, but not cold and snobby like the first. "However, may I be of any service? Is there a message you would care to leave?"

"No, thanks." My father's mouth was trembling.

I furiously tapped the card. I nodded briskly while elaborately mouthing and gesturing that he should go ahead and say his piece.

Visibly he pulled himself together. "No, wait a minute, mister. Half a tick. Aye, aye, there be a message. Tell His Royal Highness the thundering Richard Thomas works is pulling out, leaving us no work. Tell him please to stop it, mun. Tell him we are counting on him. He is trumps."

"I will convey your message to His Royal Highness." The voice was kind. "Thank you for your call. Goodbye."

My father signed off with a "Toodle-oo," remembering belatedly that "Cheerio" would have probably been more refined.

My presence of mind, urging him to declare his purpose, saved his face when he reported to his butties. He was able to compensate by saying, "If I didn't hit the bull's-eye, at least we scored a starting double."

Retelling it all, he omitted or slid over blunders and added a few trimmings. He put apocryphal remarks and promises into the secretary's mouth and aphorisms in his own. He made the whole exchange sound very smooth and elegant, as if parley with the "upper suckles" was his natural métier. By the end, he had thoroughly convinced himself that "as near a penny to four farthings" his mission was accomplished. He advised them each to write a letter to follow up his lead.

Great was his triumph when a short time afterwards, Richard Thomas & Company announced the reversal of its previous decision. They would compromise by establishing a modified version of their strip mill in the derelict steel works at Ebbw Vale. To the Prince – thus indirectly to himself for telephoning – my father gave the credit for this victory. He graciously allowed that the letters of his butties might also have contributed to this success.

Yet I knew not half a dozen of his gang put pen to paper. My father wrote, of course, guided by his former letter. Idris copied his, although not word for word – I helped him dream up half a dozen synonyms: "be glad" for "would appreciate", "desperately" for "gravely". But there was no disguising there was plagiarism or collusion somewhere.

I knew that Tich Veasey's Dad, who was practically illiterate, had Tich write a note for him. And what a specimen that must have been, Tich being practically illiterate himself. All blots and greasy fingerprints. Tich had left school at the beginning of the summer holidays. He hadn't even tried the scholarship. The ten years since he started in the Infants had gone by him as a dream. All he ever aimed for was to be a pickler like his father at the works, and nip off down to Newport every Saturday to some place near the Transporter Bridge where he had heard you could kip down with a bit of fluff and flossie for a couple of bob a fling.

Anyway, that made three letters, and I believe my Uncle Jack wrote one, probably a single sentence – he wrote as briefly as he spoke. There would certainly have been a tidy one from Obie, who should have had a better job than annealing at the works. Perhaps Ted Swilling dropped a penny postcard, coached by Hester James, his wife, who used to be a schoolteacher.

But they and the Prince did not deserve the credit any less than Prime Minister Stanley Baldwin. When announcing the decision in the Commons in October, he hogged the laurels for himself.

CHAPTER 9
WINTER, 1935

Before the year turned, my father's gladness turned to ashes. Four incidents occurred to make him militant. Three involved physical injury. First, Ruby Jones's father died from heat stroke at the works. It made my father conscious of his transience and vulnerability. Life was frighteningly short, too short to squander in a living hell – the brutalizing confines of that fiery, jangling, dangerous works – for wages that could keep his loved ones in no more than squalid poverty.

The second was an accident he had himself. A lick of flame spewed from the furnace, singed his forelock, eyelashes and eyebrows, and scorched his eyes. The doctor ordered him to wear a blindfold bandage until they healed. For weeks I had to lead him everywhere he went.

As if the physical discomfort and the fear for his sight wasn't worry enough, he had to fight for workman's compensation, poor pittance that it was. Idleness did nothing for his peace of mind. He couldn't read or garden. He could only sit and brood. His thoughts turned in and fed upon themselves.

The third concerned our Muriel. At the beginning of November we received word that she'd scalded her hand. Her employers were sure that we would rather have her come home to recuperate. If you read between those smarmy lines, you saw that a kitchen maid who couldn't use her hand was, in my father's words, "damn small use" to them. He bitterly observed, "Cheaper and less bother to write her off the payroll till she can pull her weight again." Domestics weren't covered by the workman's "comp" and sick pay was unheard of.

"Never rains but it do pour," my mother wailed as she scraped together the fares for her and me to go and fetch our Muriel home. A bus trip and a whole day off from school would normally have sent me spinning into seventh heaven. But the prospect of having my gormless sister on my hands again bowed me with anxiety.

I'd had a carefree summer with her tucked away down in Penarth, where her employers had a stately seaside house. It was next-door to impossible to get into much mischief in Penarth. It was populated with genteel old fossils who would slink out of their grey stone houses when the sun appeared. They would sit all bundled up in glassed-in shelters on the pier, or take a turn along the ornamental-gardened promenade. The common, boisterous daytrippers from Cardiff and the valleys gave it a wide berth.

When she went back after the Jubilee, I had worried that Angelo might go sniffing after her. I had tried to keep tabs on him. Luckily, I passed the Lanzos' en route to catch the train to school and coming home. Evenings and weekends particularly, the Lanzos' cafe was a hangout for the village boys. Among the blokes I had run around with since I was a tot, no one ever questioned I might be any different. I was one of them. They might treat me sometimes as if I were a younger chap, a bit more innocent than them, perhaps, and curb the talk if it got raw – but not very much.

Anyway, with this access to the Lanzo Club, I could keep a wary check on Angelo.

The more I watched him, the more Angelo fascinated me. He was glib and shrewd. His words and smiling lips said one thing, his eyes another. I would have backed my cherished penknife that he didn't have a tremble of a conscience. He pinched money from the till and lifted cigarettes right under his auntie's nose. Angle, not angel, would have been a fitter name for him.

He was cruel too. Ben had an excitable little wire-haired terrier called Clem. He was supposed to keep the rats down, but Ben and his mother had made a pet of him. One day, out on the back bailey, Ben was trying to train Clem not to jump up for his supper, but to lie patiently till served. Angelo came rushing out of the backdoor towards the lavatory and stepped on the dog's paw. The dog snarled and went for Angelo. Swearing like a mad man, Angelo grabbed the little creature by a hind leg, swung him back, forth, up and over, and slammed him down on the hard brick. The dog writhed and whimpered, so damaged he had to be put down. Ben was beside himself. He let out a huge roar and turned on Angelo. But Salvadore pulled him off and held him until he quieted down.

Ben and his mother wept for days. Angelo doubled his callousness by mock-blubbering in imitation of Ben's grief. I was chilled by the way his own family seemed to fear him.

On one occasion I was rude enough to ask Mrs. Lanzo directly, "Why do you put up with him?"

Mrs. Lanzo responded only with the pain of her dark eyes and, as always, one of the boys spoke for her. Angelo was flesh and blood, Vince said, as if that explained everything.

Angelo had a powerful appeal for women. And not just those like Elsie Fisher, who my mother called the "disgrace of womanhood". One day when I went in Turner's bike shop, I saw him chatting to Alf's wife, Nance Turner. She was old Bowles the chemist's daughter, and no dud. Nance was saying, "I don't think much of what your precious Mussolini is doing to the poor old Abyssinians, whatever miracles he's done for you Italians. That poison blister gas they spray from aeroplanes is wicked stuff."

While Alf went out to fetch our battery that he'd been recharging, Angelo replied, "The strong must be cruel to the weak in order to be kind, *carina*. In love as well as war." Out of the corner of my eye, I saw him run his finger hickory-dickory-dockwise up the inside of her arm.

I might have thought no more about it, except the following Tuesday, finishing my homework early, I happened to drop down to Lanzos' for a gas. Routinely I asked Ben, "Where is Angelo tonight?"

"Gone for a ride on our Sal's bike."

"Oh, aye." It wasn't likely he would pedal to Penarth and back.

Ben added, "That's if he can get a battery. The light was almost gone."

"Oh, aye," I said again, this time all ears. "Where would he get a battery this time of night?"

With money being short and business poor, Alf was always willing to oblige a person after hours. But Alf played the trumpet in the Pontbran Fireman's Band, and this was Tuesday, their regular rehearsal night. So a detour on my way home later seemed like a good idea. It confirmed my hunch. Sal's bike was nestled in the bushes in the lane behind the Turners' shop.

Tich corroborated my suspicions when we next met on the back lane. Since Tich had joined the throng of uninsured adolescents waiting vainly for a job, he had found nothing better to fill the heavy-hanging hours than to shadow Angelo. He would have given both his squinty little squirrel's eyes to be like him.

Tich had recently entertained us with a different slant on Angelo. We learned from him that the black rigout that Angelo wore wasn't any kind of native costume, like the turbans worn by Indians down Tiger Bay or the scarlet fezzes of the Bute Street Turks. No, Tich informed us, the black shirt was a uniform. The toughs Angelo ran around with also wore them, underneath their overcoats. Tich thought the organization they attended down in Newport might be some sort of an adult Boy Scouts.

To check out his theory, Tich pilfered change for bus fare from his mother's purse one evening. He came back frenzied with excitement. The account he gave us was so garbled and fantastic, it sounded like a toasted-cheese-and-pickle-onion-supper dream. For quite a while he went round throwing out his arm and goose-stepping. Then suddenly he froze up solid on the subject and would only tell us escapades by Angelo of the strictly amorous variety.

Such as this about Nance Turner. Leering ghoulishly, he told us he had seen them huddled between mounds in Siloam Chapel Graveyard. Tich made various obscene gestures to describe their carryings on.

I was sorry for old Alf. I was even sorry for poor Nance. Her enormous, dark-ringed eyes and pale thin face looked as if consumption might be eating her away. But I was glad for me. It wasn't very likely Angelo would spend hard-to-come-by money going to Penarth on spec, when there was plenty of entertainment to be had in his own bailiwick.

When I accompanied my mother to fetch our Muriel home, I saw at once I could save myself the worry of her being in his reach again. It was clear she'd be in no condition to go sparking for a bit. Her hand was swathed in bandage to the elbow, and her pretty face so drawn, it even gave me quite a pang. Tired out as well as hurt, she was. They worked them fifty hours a week and more in those big houses and my sister wasn't any too robust. Though you never heard her grumbling.

We were summoned to the drawing room by the lady of the house. "It was the poshest house I've ever been in," I told Bryn and Ruby afterwards, "and the closest I have ever come to any toff." She had been a handsome woman in her time. White-haired now, but straight, tall and willowy. Taller even than my father. And fine teeth, all her own.

Growing up, I had soaked in all those attitudes that we now call discrimination against such people as the black men down the docks, or the ochre, slant-eyed herbalist called Chin-Chin-Chow, whose brews my Grandma swore by for her palpitations and her joints. But I compared my little old squat Mam, stunted by undernourishment all her growing years, whose current diet of mainly tea and bread-and-butter kept her pale and puffed, and whose own gapped, crooked teeth had long since crumbled and been pulled out and replaced by a china set; I compared my mother with that elegant lady and saw discrimination was a matter just as much of caste and economics as of race, sex and religion, the marks of which you bore for life. My mother's speech, her looks, her manners, would segregate her from the higher-born until she died, although she was a Protestant, although her skin was white.

That was when I started wondering which way us young ones of the working class should head. With all the certainty and cheek of twelve, I was already asking: Should we use the same old system of the takers-and-the-took, and use our education just to richen ourselves up? Or should we try to knock a bit of sense into the heads of our own sort to act together for the common good?

God knew, they needed it. For the fourth incident that opened my father's hitherto forbearing eyes and made him militant, was the incredible stupidity of the vast majority of his fellow countrymen. They were utterly incapable of seeing and pursuing their own interest. When the government went to the people and the people went to the polls that November, 1935, the Conservative Party was returned to power with a whopping great majority. Not even the naive Americans were that obtuse; they at least had had the sense to put in Roosevelt.

I had no illusions, even at that early age, about what was happening in my father's head. With his eyes so bad, I had to do his reading for him. Besides the daily papers, he had me read him pamphlets lent by Emrys Strong, who was like the bogey man always lurking in the shadows, waiting for his chance.

One evening in December, my father, still blindfolded, asked me please to lead him later to the Pontbran Orchards pub. I thought at first he meant to bend his elbow at the public bar. But at teatime, he ate only two bites of his favourite brawn before offering it to me. For the remainder of the meal he sat in deep, tooth-picking thought. My mother had to boss him to let her drop oil in his eyes and bind them up again.

In a disused, barn-like room at the back of the pub's skittle alley, my father had convened a "mass" meeting of his butties and acquaintances. The proceedings were punctuated by the thuds of balls colliding with the pins. The hall adjoined a pigsty too, so the stink was fierce.

The turnout was impressive. Our Dad kicked off the meeting without ceremony or delay. "I have taken the liberty to call us all together to give us chance to air our bitterness and thrash this matter out." He was referring to the hostile government put once more at the helm. Above the black bandanna he wore over his bandages, his forehead gleamed, although the temperature was perishing. "At least *this* privilege is left to us in this benighted land: to air our grievances and disappointments – if only to the flaming wind."

Obie Dixon said, "I am a reasonable man. I'm patient and forgiving. But this last bit of folly at the ballot box is beyond my ken." His gentle face and prudent disposition were all thrown out of shape with unaccustomed chagrin. "Labour's goose is cooked for good," he said.

A ritual chorus of "Hear-hear, hear-hear," kept rippling through the group.

Nwd Probert shook his crinkled head. "No, don't say that," he pleaded. His life's mission was to fan the faintest hope to make the vale of tears endurable.

"At least for many years to come," Perce Cook declared. "The stigma of MacDonald will be hard to fade."

"They'll have to have a new election in five years, though, won't they?" Tich Veasey's father said.

Emrys gave a mocking laugh. "And what is to become of us meanwhile?" Out poured his usual tirade. "You thought yourselves so bloody clever helping to keep Richard Thomas in South Wales. But you did bugger all to stop them replacing flesh and blood with shiny new machines. Smart business, that. Half our jobs will soon be gone."

Ted Swilling timidly enquired, "Won't the Special Areas Program do anything to stop it, mun?"

Coarse laughter rocked the rafters, loosening showers of dust. The pigs began to squeal. Emrys said, "Where you been to, Ted? Didn't you see the Commissioner's first report? How his hands were tied, he said? How the programme wasn't nearly what it was cracked up to be?"

Perce Cook called out, "Won't Hester teach you how to read, Ted?" It was a standing joke how a dunce like Ted could have landed himself a teacher for a wife. There was more laughter and more falling dust at Perce's sarkiness and Ted's embarrassment.

Few others were in any doubt what a massive hoax the government had perpetrated on them with the Special Areas Act. None of Commissioner Malcolm Stewart's suggestions had been heeded during the year that it had, so-say, been in force. It was time, Emrys said, to realize what a sop, what a dummy teat they had been handed, to keep them quiet in their prams. But even a brainless baby soon found out when no milk was coming through.

"Emrys is right," my father suddenly spoke up in ringing tones. Everyone was galvanized to prickling attention. Never in their memory had they heard Fred Williams back up Emrys Strong. Had Emrys swung him round at last?

"Emrys is right," my father said again. "The Richard Thomas affair teaches us big money can pull the plug on us any time they have a bloody mind. And like Emrys says, the Special Bloody Areas Act is a mockery."

The pause that followed was electric. You could hear a piglet sigh.

I had been watching Emrys as my father talked. His smirk turned to a grin of triumph. "Tell them, Fred," he urged. "All the power the British worker's got is to yap and harp a bit to try to prod their masters. But they always keep us where they want us, at the bottom of the heap. The Soviet people have offensive power, not this defensive rearguard action stuff. The proletariat got cracking and did something positive to improve their lot."

Emrys looked back from the audience to my father, offering him the floor to declare and pledge himself for the CP.

But quick as a whip, my father said, "Except, Em, this ent the bloody Soviet Union we be living in, look, is it? And however bloody blind they be, the majority in this democracy *did* go into the ballot booth to take their pick. It is their privilege to act like bloody dunces if they want. There ent no law against them hurting their own selves by voting daft."

He took a deep breath and dramatically changed key. "Besides, there is one mighty benefit we still possess the Bolshies don't: Us minority is still loose on the countryside. Still able to protest. Not locked up in some clink or banished to Siberia."

Emrys's expression of bewilderment turned rapidly to fury. "Then what the hell's this meeting all about? We should have stayed home in the warm."

My father's whole demeanour turned sombre with authority. Before my eyes, he grew in stature as an orator, "There are other roads to action besides going Communist. In the dark I may have been these past few weeks. But not without enlightenment. What came to me is this. These many years we've been a loyal band. Every time I put forward my idea to get the Prince to be our spokesman, you've rallied round. And he has always backed us up and been our champion. It is not his fault the Special Areas Act's a sham. Nor that the Richard Thomas thing is such a farce."

My father rubbed his hand across his blindfold as though to wipe the mist out of his eyes. "So what I am proposing, mates, is this. Let us band together – found a permanent organisation. Ready at a minute's notice to petition the Prince, enlist his aid. And even if there is a limit to the things that he can do for us, he will be there as a symbol of better times to come. A lighthouse in the fog to keep us going." His voice dropped in tone but not in volume, to a level of highest seriousness. "Let us form an Order, a Brotherhood, we can be proud of. Joined together in a noble cause."

"So help me, you make sense, Fred," Obie Dixon breathed.

And that is how the Loyal Order of the Prince of Wales was born.

CHAPTER 10
DECEMBER 1935 TO JANUARY 1936

There were those who jeered at the Order, calling it flash-in-the-pan and kiddy-games. But in the few short weeks between its conception in December and the grand initiation ceremony early in January 1936, applications for memberships were double the basic core of loyal butties.

There were several surprises. After all his static, Emrys wanted to belong.

"Why do you let him in, our Dad?" I asked.

"For all his miserable cantankerousness, he is our butty, love. And no one takes him seriously. He is nothing but a bag of hotted wind. Likes to raise a stink just for the sheer sake of it." Obie had once gone so far as to predict that if Emrys ever saw his Communist goals attained, he'd switch to something opposite. His natural habitat was ferment and unrest. Only in a warring context did he feel at peace.

Emrys also served the group as devil's advocate. Even if listing to one side, his mind was sharp. Moreover, my father said, "It is wise to have him in a place where we can watch him. Always mingle with your enemy, Vid, to know what they are at. Don't drive them underground where they can undermine your house."

Another big surprise was Angelo. He claimed the right to be included as the Prince was interested in Italy's political experiments. Even more surprising, Emrys nominated him. "By damn, that is a puzzler, them two to share a trough," my father said. Germany, Japan and Italy were already ganging up against the Soviet Union.

"They've been getting pretty thick," I said. I had often seen them chinwagging at Lanzos' and caught snatches of their arguments when I sat at the next table.

"Benito Mussolini is a modern saviour," said Angelo in one exchange.

"That bloody fascist?!" Emrys screeched. "Aih, get away with you!"

"At least he saved our country without the bloodbath like your Bolshies caused. My father was in a *squadre* in the March on Rome. He vouched no shot was fired. The King handed the country to *Il Duce* on a plate. That's genius."

I went to help Ben take out the rubbish and catch up on his news. They were still at it when I got back. I ignored Bryn Thomas's account of a fine punt at a recent rugby match and peeled my ears to pick up more of Angelo's skilled double talk.

Emrys was saying, "I'm blowed. So those corporations are really labour syndicates." He rubbed his withered arm. "Before the war I was strong for Tom Mann. More on Trotsky's side until they ran him out. I still would rather workers directly own their trades and industry than have state centralization but . . ." He shrugged.

Angelo leaned back self-importantly, "What would you think of a system that used the best of both? *Il Duce* says the State is Everything. But he set up the Great Council of *Corporazioni,* too. You might feel very much at home with that."

I wanted to keep listening, but Bryn jerked my arm. "Come on, mun. Old as we are, we will get tanned backsides if we're late again."

There were other occasions when I eavesdropped on Angelo's political seductions. He was a master at turning everything his way. Even when the fascists and the communists progressed towards the trial of strength of the

Spanish Civil War, Angelo craftily played down the clash. "What's your church, Em?"

"My church? Name of God, religion is against my principles."

"I know. But just for the sake of talking, how you were brought up."

"Say Baptist. That is where the old dutch goes."

"Now me, I'm reared a Catholic. There are two religions at each other's throat. Yet they're both Christian. See what I am driving at?"

"Keep going."

"When you put them up against real opposites like the Hindus or the Moslems, you see how close they really are. Fascism and communism are at bottom just the same. Blood brothers squabbling. This degenerate capitalist class society of England is far more opposite to each of us than us to one another." You could learn a lot from Angelo about shrewd argument.

Oddly enough, other unlikely applicants for membership in the Loyal Order were recruits of my mother. Her reaction to the creation of the group had been a more-than-usually extravagant performance of long-suffering. But chance worked with certain quirks in her personality to help her enlist a couple of individuals who would play crucial parts in later actions of the company.

Dearer than all the Welsh gold in the royal coffers was my Mam to me. So no disrespect is meant to say I had her pegged quite early on. I agreed with my father that "she flapped the bit of gristle in her mouth too much" and "put her snout in where it wasn't wanted, thank you very much." He privately advised me to regard her long nose and double-jointed tongue as incurable handicaps and to resign myself to them as he had had to do. He always made such observations in good humour. I had no doubts about their bond.

My mother was extremely chapelly. My father was raised in the Church of England and, almost as bad, had become agnostic when he reached his spiritual majority. So you had to wonder what my mother ever saw in him.

She went religiously to chapel every Sunday evening. When she was crammed into her Sunday corset like lead into a bullet, and was attired in floral print, with her hair done up in smooth tight sausages, row upon rigid row, like a judge's wig; when she had her hat on, and her gloves stroked snug into the crotches of her fingers, she looked as though a harsh word never passed her lips.

This combination of my mother's garrulousness and chapel-habit made a founding member out of Twm Sion Griffiths. We happened to run into him at a Christmas tableau and carol service at the Congregational Chapel, which we visited to hear my cousin sing.

All I knew about Twm Sion Griffiths previously was that he was one of the men my mother threw at my father when she claimed she could have had her pick of half a dozen better natured and more prosperous than he. I gathered Mr. Griffiths had, once upon a distant time, been sweet on her. Though he was a decade older than her if a day.

It was hilarious to watch a tough old bantam like my mother go giggly-girlish at Twm Sion Griffiths' boyish eagerness. A less romantic pair it would have been impossible to find. Twm Sion was barely an inch and a pepper her superior, with a head like a china egg set in the straw to hoax-coax the hens to lay. He also had a tubby little tummy whose only virtue was that it set off his gold watch and chain.

He was very "Welshy" in his speech, full of "looks" and "sees". Until he went to school, apparently, he had only spoken Welsh, and if he had his way we would all be talking nothing else. He always used the Welsh spelling of his name: "Twm Sion Gruffydd, Sanitary Engineer" adorned the cornice of his shop.

Anyway, as he left his pew, he exclaimed, "Well, well, fancy seeing you down here, look, Mrs. Williams!"

"Mr. Griffiths! Well I never!" my mother minced.

I tripped over a hymn book that had fallen in the aisle, and said, "Oh, blow!" as befitted hallowed premises. His eyes looked daggers, as if I had said foul language. I wondered what his reaction would have been if, instead of catching myself up sharp, I had let rip with my usual ripe expletives.

I knew my mother itched to box me a ringing clout, but she could do nothing more than glower in the circumstances. To cover her discomposure, she became sociably effusive and gave her tongue its head. "I haven't seen you for this long time, Mr. Griffiths. I don't know when it was the last."

"No, not this long time, Mrs. Williams, is it? Several years, I bet."

"And how have you been keeping?"

"Fighting fit, I thank you, may the Lord be praised. Nothing much to grumble at, mind. And your own good self?"

"Not at all bad, thank you. Just the usual ups and downs. But there's a lot we can be thankful for."

"The Lord is good."

"He is indeed."

"And this here is your youngest girl? She've grown."

"She won the scholarship and doing well." I was surprised to find her showing pride in me.

"And how is Mr. Williams, look?"

"Fred's fit to middling, thank you, Mr. Griffiths. Keeping very busy with one thing and another."

"I saw it in the *Argus* he was made secretary of the British Legion not so long ago." He was just a hairbreadth short of snotty, so I knew he had to be teetotal too.

My mother flushed and hastened to assure him she wasn't wedded to a drunken sot. "They talked him into it. Him being an ex-serviceman. And because he writes a lovely hand." Wildly grabbing anything to build her stock, she said, "The Prince of Wales is Legion President, you know. A lovely speech he made to them last year." That triggering yet another thought, she galloped on, "As a matter of fact, Fred has got a more important office than with the Legion. He is President of a new society honouring the Prince of Wales."

I stared at her. Only a couple of hours before, after failing to persuade my father to accompany her to chapel, she had blasted him where he was most susceptible, with criticism of the Loyal Order. "You are worse than children playing pantomime. When will all this nonsense cease?"

Mr. Griffith's reaction was more than sham polite.

"It ent the Royal March on Windsor starting up again?"

"No, no. But this *grew* out of that, though, in a way."

Mr. Griffiths clucked and nodded with more than common courtesy. My mother thrived on it. She said, "They formed into a permanent sort of Lodge. They picked Fred President, it being his idea." As if the organization had had her blessing all the way, she added in hushed reverence, "The Loyal Order of The Prince of Wales, it's called."

Mr. Griffiths darted furtive looks around, drew near, and murmured in her ear, "Is it only open to the tin workers, I wonder, Missus?"

Infected by his confidential air, my mother whispered back, "Oh, no, indeed. Nwd Probert's in it. And Bill, Fred's younger brother's in the wireworks."

"Ruby Jones uncle's from the brick works," I supplied. "Barney O'Quirk is in, Nick Vowles the Baker, and even Mr. MacDour is very interested." Mr. MacDour had a drapery and tailor's shop and was a magistrate.

Like a kiddie asking for a bag of mixed boiled sweets at Truman's market stall, Mr. Griffiths said, "I wonder if they'd let a poor old plumber join?"

The way my mother's bosom swelled, I secretly predicted that the path henceforth would be a good deal smoother for my father in his doings with the Loyal Order.

Twm Sion Griffith's interest in the Loyal Order was as oblique as Barney O'Quirk's. Although born in Anglo-Welsh South Wales, Twm Sion was a Welshman to the bone. He hated the English with a sullen, smouldering intensity. He hated them for putting down Owain Glyndwr in the fifteenth century and spelling the doom of Wales as a separate Principality. He hated them for the way their Robber Barons exploited the minerals and defaced his pleasant land, and for the neglect of Welsh workers by Tory Parliaments before and since the War. Being a stern Nonconformist "chapel" man, he hated them for the snobbery and moral flabbiness of the English Church. And being a pacifist, he hated them for always tangling in wars and conscripting the reluctant, peace-loving Welsh into the fray to do their dirty work.

In politics, Twm Sion revealed obsessive single-mindedness: Wales for the Welsh. He was a zealous supporter of Plaid Cymru, the Welsh Nationalist Party. As such, you'd expect him to repudiate the Prince as a scion of the English Crown and Church. In fact, he admired him as a rebel of those institutions. He saw *this* Royal Highness as just the type to throw his weight behind a movement of Home Rule for Wales. The Prince was Twm Sion's choice to head up the new "Dominion".

When my mother found what boons my father's nonsense could confer on her, even putting old flames in her debt, she began to publicize the Order widely. She went around inviting everyone and anyone to join, including some my father would as soon not have had to bother with.

One such was Clarence Makepiece, who had been gassed at Mons – or maybe it was shell-shocked on the Marne. In either case, he was said to have a steel plate in his head. When the war was over, he had taken to strong drink. Although, before his injuries, he had been a good Wesleyan, the deacons had been forced, they claimed, to cast him out. "There is Christianity for you," my father said, "to spit on somebody when they are down." When Clarence later saw the light and swore off booze, he started his own holy-roller chapel, affiliated with the Spiritualistic Apostolic Church of Pentecost. My father applauded him for not crawling back to the Wesleyans. Not that my father approved of the narrow bigotry and silly literalism and fundamentalism of the newer sects. He simply endorsed their break from the former split-offs, which had, in their turn, become too settled and respectable. Any show of spunk and independence won his admiration.

Clarence and his wife had built their shed-like chapel next door to my Granddad's. We would sit out on the lawn on summer evenings and hear the ructions going on across the hedge. Clarence's flock responded to his pulpit-bellowing with tumultuous "Hallelujahs" and "Amens". Sometimes, in the middle of a sermon or a prayer, someone would be moved to start a hymn, and in a twinkling the whole congregation took it up. Sometimes somebody would cry or moan, and the entire gathering would follow suit. They would work themselves up into a frantic fury of religious mania, and end up rock-and-rolling in the aisles.

So when my mother recruited Clarence for the Loyal Order, my father told me confidentially, "Him's one we could have done without." But it was not his nature to turn anyone away.

The crowd who met in the back room of the British Legion that first week of January to be officially inducted into the Loyal Order were a motley crew in looks as in ideas.

The initiation was a liberal adaptation of the investiture of the Prince of Wales at Caernarvon Castle almost a quarter of a century before. The mantle placed in turn around each pledge's shoulders was the Welsh Red Dragon. Twm Sion never tired of reminding us it was the standard of Cadwaladr, last king of Southern Britain – Prydain being what Wales was called before the invasion and occupation of the English. The actual flag was the one my mother blew her corset money on for the Silver Jubilee. It had been gathering dust behind my washstand since the corps' return from Cardiff.

For ceremonial sword, Ted Swilling lent his scimitar-shaped knife looted from a Gurkha corpse in the Mesopotamian campaign. The symbolic Ring and Rod were curtain hardware from Powell-the-Ironmonger's shop. Those poor imitations were a far cry from the rich regalia of royalty. Yet they radiated their own aura of majesty and grace.

Since my father's eyes were almost healed, I was no longer needed as his guide. But I had become a kind of habit as automatically accepted as Austen Bishop's sheepdog, who went everywhere with him, even to the works. I was as good as an honorary member, but I conducted myself as a self-effacing acolyte, watching for my cues from the shadows in the wings.

Each pledge received three twine-bound white hen's feathers, after the Prince's emblem, as each swore his oath "*Ich Dien*" – I Serve – all foreign imports of heraldic lore, of which we were all blithely unaware.

A cynic might have thought the whole thing farcical. But it was a vital and electric evening. An aura of genuine solemnity pervaded the theatrical proceedings. It elevated the pathetic and the shabby into something almost spiritual and beautiful.

Clarence Makepiece bawled "Amen" and "Praise the Lord" every whip stitch. Twm Sion Gruffydd, catching fire, thundered, "*Gogoniant*," the Welsh for glory, and "*Cymru am Byth*" – "Wales for Ever". More conventional types cried, "Hear, hear", "Well done" and joined in Angelo's "Bravo" as the spirit moved. The mystic fervour and the cloven tongues suggested a mighty rushing wind was in the offing.

The obligatory singing was inspired. Under Nwd's animated baton, the swell and harmony of "Bread of Heaven, Feed me now and evermore," made a lump come in my throat. They sang, "Among our Ancient Mountains, and through our lovely vales/Oh, let the prayer re-echo, God Bless the Prince of Wales" with a sweetness and sincerity that brought tears to my eyes. "*Mae Hen Wlad*" was never rendered with more heart.

After the installation was completed, all the members of the Loyal Order filed into the bar to celebrate. So rousing was the camaraderie that even Twm Sion Gruffydd lingered to partake of a small beer. They parked me in the corner like a seeing-eye dog. But Clarence Makepiece was eased out of the door, not to tempt him off the wagon and get the Order off to a bad start.

CHAPTER 11
JANUARY, 1936

What happened next threatened to render obsolete the Loyal Order of the Prince of Wales the moment she came off the slips. On January 17 1936, that venerable gentlemen, King George the Fifth, took desperately ill in Sandringham.

We sat glued to the wireless, waiting for this tough, independent character to yield his ghost. It was as though the nation stood in the antechamber to his bedroom solemnly watching the closed doors, while the old king did defiant battle with his destiny. For the first time the common people were in at a royal death where only the nobility had been allowed before.

Hour after hour on the quarter, the BBC announcer chanted mournfully, "The King's life is moving to its close." We couldn't bear to listen. We had to stick it out until we knew.

The end came on January 20 1936. They said that it was the falling of a sacred oak. "I didn't hear or feel no thud myself," my father said. He wouldn't. His ears were filled with the sound of heralds' trumpets proclaiming Edward King.

My mother mourned as though it was a close relation who had passed away. She grieved as though a deluge was pent up inside her. Courage and good taste would only let a trickle through a tiny sluice, to guard against the lock-gate giving way.

For days on end the wireless news was taken up with details of the lying in state, condolences, and finally the funeral itself. It would have gone on even longer had Edward not requested a shorter period to display the coffin in Westminster Abbey than Church and Cabinet preferred.

My father stomached it so long, then said, "Sorry the old bugger has pegged out, and all. But let's keep a bit of balance, is it?"

"You cruel, heartless sod." My mother shook a thwarted fist at him.

"It is time the nation turned to think on him who's landed in the old man's boots. The King be dead. Long live the King."

The Prince's elevation paradoxically deepened my father's empathy with him. The thoughts of most of us dwelt on the corpse rolling on the gun carriage from Sandringham to Westminster, on the catafalque past which a million loyal subjects filed, and on the coffin as it was dead-marched off to Windsor. My father walked in spirit beside the slight, bowed figure who, escorted, guarded, followed his dead father in the obsequies of state.

There was nothing presumptuous in my father's feelings that he and his sovereign were one spirit in two bodies. King Edward was a man of privilege; yet he lacked political authority. He had rank without a vote. My father, theoretically had the rights and privileges of political responsibility, yet was dirt poor and powerless. He believed that if he and his royal counterpart could only pool their assets, their liabilities would cancel each other out, and a perfect world would be achieved.

Disposing of my father's personal effects after his death, I came across the mildewed Loyal Order's Minute Book. At the first meeting following King George's death, the President addressed the membership in moving terms, taking as his "text" a newspaper cutting, "This socially-conscious monarch (Edward VIII) will span the yawning gap between the people and their government, and give compelling expression to the truly popular will." A unanimous motion expressed the feeling that the Loyal Order's mission was stronger than ever. The name's anachronism was resolved: "There being no heir to title of the Prince of Wales, we are all for keeping Edward on that job as well as being King. So therefore be it resolved this Order be ordained the Loyal, Royal Order of the Prince of Wales, His Majesty King Edward VIII."

A neat marginal addendum confirmed their choice. "In his first St. David's Day address as King he said, 'You know me as Prince of Wales, and that is who I shall always be.'"

The book also served as a scrap book and as a diary-cum-notebook. There were many clippings pasted between recordings of the minutes. "In the heart of the King, the distress of those who suffer takes foremost place whether due to war or tragic consequence of unemployment."

"A democrat by taste and sympathy, manly and self-respecting, dignified without haughtiness, simple and unpretentious in demeanor, never holding himself aloof from the common life, regarding himself not as the master, but as the tireless servant of the people."

There were various notes in my father's hand. "I have heard some people call him Ned the Meddler, and King Ed the Red. Sticks and stones can break his bones but names can never hurt him."

Then came a list, headed, "He will go down in history as:
Edward the Innovator
The Reformer
The Fair
The Democrat
The Just
The King with the Common Touch
The King who Took Our Part."
Examples followed. "Remember how he saluted the

untouchables in Bombay, and the Zulus in Natal. The world loves and respects him for speaking out for them. He will do the same for us."

Several pictures also graced the Minute Book. One was of the King making the St. David's Day address, his first speech as King to the country and the Empire. In the margin was a note: the King had broken with tradition by addressing his subjects as, "My fellow men."

The King was depicted attending church services in celebration of the Welsh Guards' coming of age on St. David's Day. These Welsh connections had doubled our pleasure as we heard about them on the radio and in the press.

The picture of the new King visiting the Chelsea Flower Show was particularly endearing to my father, who yearned to see that horticultural wonder.

Another picture was the King inspecting the new super-liner the Queen Mary on the Clyde before it sailed on its first transatlantic voyage. The slump had interrupted its completion, but now it was being touted as the symbol of economic recovery.

This trip to Scotland was the first of the King's promised visits to outlying depressed places in his kingdom. On his way to Clydebank, he was taken to the Glasgow slums to inspect a rehousing project. He rattled the Establishment by commenting, "How do you reconcile the world that has produced this mighty ship with the slums we have just visited?"

The King's remark was manna to my father. It validated all the Loyal Order's faith. My father predicted, "As God is my judge, he'll come to see us here before the year is out. It stands to reason, after our phone call and the letters, he will think of us."

His quiet conviction suggested he had far more definite

intelligence than mere inference or surmise. It was as though he and the King were connected by a speaking tube.

I had already taken on some of my mother's skepticism about my father's mumpy. But never to laugh at it or show him disrespect. For me, his mumpy was a valuable study course in practical politics – a long field trip with hands-on experience never offered in any school. Besides, we got a lot of fun out of the suspense it generated in our impoverished world. But would we ever have the fun and wonder of seeing our Sovereign up close?

CHAPTER 12
SPRING TO SUMMER, 1936

I had my plate full swotting for end-of-term exams in May and June. That was how I came to miss the budding of the next phase of the mumpy. I don't know when I twigged that something big was brewing. I think I sensed a sea change in my father's mood. He was like an E string strung tight enough to cut into a fiddle bridge. I tried various dodges to fish information out of him, but he was not forthcoming.

Once a year I accompanied my mother to Ty-Trappa Farm to measure Mrs. Pickford for the couple of summer frocks my mother annually "ran up" for her. Mrs. Pickford was an eighteen-stone tub of slopping lard. Her son, Gib Pickford, was our milkman. Whenever I visited the farm I would wear my Wellingtons and help him feed the chickens and serve the pigs their swill. Gib was on the half-baked side. His teeth were like a higgledy-piggledy ring of cromlech stones. His hair stuck out like sun-dried thatch. The milkman's overall he always wore hung on him like a bumpkin's smock. He was just the sort of bloke that you could tap for secrets without him catching on to what you were up to. I aimed to coax this newest gossip out of him.

When he was comfortably settled squirting milk, I said, "You glad you joined the Loyal Order, Gib?" He had joined because the workless were obliged, ironically, to *cut back* their milk order when they brought another mouth into the world. At the rate things were going, his milk round would soon be more like a charitable organisation than a business. He preferred to give his milk away than throw it in the gutter when it soured.

I rephrased my question, "Do you think the Loyal Order is a good idea?"

"Oh, aye," he said delightedly. "It is a bit of fun."

"I expect you are excited about this new development."

"What's that?" He appeared genuinely puzzled.

"You know!" I chided jocularly, implying I knew better than to mention it right out.

"Oh, aye," he nodded, obviously tumbling to what he thought I meant.

"Our Dad been telling me about it, mun. Very confidential. There's marvelous, en it?"

"Aye, marvelous." He leered conspiratorially.

"What do you feel about it, Gib?"

He tugged rhythmically for half a minute. The stream pinged against the bucket side. "He won't half be surprised."

"Not half he won't."

"I bet nothing ever happened to him like that before."

"I bet it didn't!"

"He won't mind when we explain, though."

"Naih, he won't mind," I said.

"And when he sees we don't mean any harm."

"No harm at all."

"After all, we got as much right as the bigwigs have to chat with our King."

Hoarsely, I said, "We do, indeed."

"Even if the only way to do it is to nab him on the sly."

"Nab him on the sly," I echoed weakly.

He was quiet for a while, wobbling the udders. I swallowed hard. To confirm this startling information, I remarked, "It will take some doing, the way he's guarded."

"Uh?" Gib said. It only took him a second to catch up. "Aye. It en gonna be easy to corner him, get him on his own. But us'll do our best."

"When's this gonna happen, Gib?"

He stopped tugging momentarily and looked at me askance. I had forgotten to frame my question to sound as if I was already in the know. He reminded me, "Like the paper reckoned, he'll come sometime in the autumn."

I hurried to say, "Yes, of course." But how had I missed reading such an item? Why had I not heard my father comment on it?

Gibby got up and moved the stool and frothy bucket to another cow.

As soon as he was settled, I peered with alarm towards the far end of the barn. "What's that?"

"What's what?" He paled a little.

"I thought I heard a noise."

We exchanged scared glances.

"Naih," he said. "Couldn't've been." But still he had to check to satisfy himself.

When he returned, I said, "I was afraid it might be someone eavesdropping. You never know. It is risky even to discuss these things between ourselves, I s'pose. Our Dad would break my back if he found out that I talked to you. You wouldn't cop on me," I begged.

"Nor you on me, mun. We could both get in hot water."

"We better keep our mouths shut from now on."

So there it was. The newest and most daring plan was somehow, somewhere, to waylay the Royal Personage to gain the Royal Ear.

That wasn't the only tidbit I picked up that day. When Gib and I went in to tea, we were just in time to hear the name of Nancy Turner drop.

Mrs. Pickford, stuffing scones, the butter dribbling down her chin, was saying, "They say she went to Coventry."

"Her sister's there, the nurse," my mother said.

"More like it she is gone to be a patient at her sister's

hospital, if you ask me. There's summat very wrong about that girl. Summat is corroding her insides. I have said it for a long time, look."

My mother said, "Hearing this about her dirty ways, you wonder if it ent –" Catching sight of me, she left the sentence dangling. She made very busy straightening the tea cozy.

Mrs. Pickford refused to forfeit a good gossip on my account. She said, "Her Dad been doling out the arsenic for years. You'd think he could have taken care of her." Nance Turner's father was Jim Bowles the Chemist.

My mother muttered, "I expect she let it go too far, the wicked hussy." She pointed me a place to sit, making warning signals with her eyes and brows for me to please behave myself.

"Who's that?" said Gibby, working his way round the shabby Victorian clutter that strewed the way from door to hearth.

"I've been telling Mrs. Williams what you heard about the Turners, Gib."

"En it a shame," Gib said, removing pin cushion and inch-tape from his horsehair chair. "Everybody've known this long time how old Nance been carrying on. Everybody 'cept poor Alf."

"Never heard a word myself," my mother said resentfully. "Who told Alf, finally?"

"Angelo got over-excited talking politics in the Oddfellows. Let it drop that he and Nance had arguments about it. The cat jumped out of the bag by accident."

I flashed on an image of Angelo boasting about both the fall of Addis Ababa and Nance in the same breath.

Mrs. Pickford said, "Alf will divorce her, I expect."

"Tch, tch," my mother said, clutching the frill around her throat. "She have done wrong, admitted. But *that* is not the way to settle it. I don't hold with divorce. It ent nothing but a dodge for men to wiggle out of their responsibilities."

Mrs. Pickford nodded. "Too true. Especially when they're saddled with a bunch of little mouths to feed in these hard times. It isn't *Christian* to up and leave."

Gib said, "Then how about that Blodwyn Paul divorcing Cliff?" That was the sole divorce in our community for many years. "The way he run around, she had good cause."

"Never," said my mother. "It is bad enough a man thinking to divorce his wife, whatever the cause. But it is inexcusable for a woman to divorce her husband. You can *expect* men to philander, the dirty lot. It is the cross us women have to bear. But it is no grounds to break the bonds of holy matrimony."

We would soon discover that this harsh moral standard among the womenfolk, which allowed their sex no quarter, shook thrones and toppled monarchs. And did so faster and more ruthlessly than if the monarch had himself been charged with lechery or tyranny.

Unlike the plan for the Royal-March-on-Windsor, this latest variation on my father's mumpy – to accost the King – gave him little pleasure. His mood grew more sombre. I suspected that he looked upon it as a wretched, dangerous duty, like reconnoitering at the front. The Loyal Order might have strong justification and the highest moral purpose, but as a realist and responsible citizen, my father knew that it was bound to be regarded as sedition or some other highly suspect crime against the Crown. It would make no difference that they revered and cherished every blond to greying hair of their dear monarch's head. They would be treated as a menace and summarily dealt with, if they got too close to him. Only my father's sense of brotherhood with his uncrowned king, together with his courage and imagination, could break that barrier.

All through the summer, I learned later, he hoped against hope there would be an upturn in the valley's fate so he could call the tactic off. But things did not get better. Indeed, the unemployment level in South Wales worsened in comparison to the country as a whole. Nobody should have expected any different – the Conservative Baldwin had assumed the premiership from MacDonald in mid-1935.

Because of the changeover in sovereigns, Commissioner Malcolm Stewart's second report of January 1936 had gone largely unnoticed. It had painted as pitiful a picture of the nation's blackspots as his first. He had offered a long list of strong recommendations. But the Government made a mockery of them with a couple of weak, placating legislative moves. It was clearly marking time until the Special Areas Act ran out nine months ahead.

Disgust at such betrayal hardened the defiant hearts of members of the Loyal Order and stiffened their resolve. They knew they would gain nothing from a government of aristocrat-conservatives without taking risks. They would approach their paragon at any cost.

The hardest part was waiting. They had no definite event or date on which to train their nervous energy. Even their conviction that the King was shortly coming to South Wales was based only on a tentative hypothesis. Odds on he wouldn't come.

Never a patient man, my father verged on apoplexy throughout those creeping, aching months.

"Fred! What is wrong with you?" my mother reprimanded him. "You are always flying off the handle at the slightest thing."

He took testy action, such as rapping the wall with the poker knob if the Davies's wireless got a bit too loud. Several times on night shift, he flung up the bedroom sash and, leaning out in his nightshirt, swore flashes at the children playing tag. "Don't you know that some poor buggers have to sleep days? Get the hell away from here. Go and do your brawling in your own backyard."

He would hate himself for letting his quick temper get the best of him, especially turning nasty on the little ones. "My bloody nerves be shot to buggery," he pleaded for excuse.

My mother said, "I expect you need a tonic, Fred. Some yeast or iron tablets. Your blood is thin."

"Thin blood be damned. Fit as a fiddle am I, except for this here heartburn. It is too much fry-up we've been having lately. That is the cause of that."

"Indeed it isn't! You march off down and see old Dr. Evans if your thundering stomach is that sensitive."

My father seldom visited the doctor, nor did the doctor visit him. There was a weekly stoppage from his pay-packet for hospital and doctors, so he was entitled to their services. But he didn't have much faith in them.

However, work rules required a follow-up visit to the surgery to check his recovery from the scorching accident. As Dr. Evans peered with his light into his eyes, my father casually asked, "Would you happen to have summat that would move the wind?"

"What's the trouble, Mr. Williams?"

"My guts is all unsettled. I sometimes think my flaming brains is in my stomach. Every time I have to use my head, my bile is churned."

He got some pungent, chalky stuff. Whenever he took a swig, "There's good!" he'd say, marvelously relieved,

He carried a small bottle in his pocket, and grew to be a proper toper of the stuff. He quaffed it much as Ted Swilling nipped gin from his pewter flask. My father sent me down for several refills. Fortunately, it was surgery-dispensed, not on prescription from the Chemist, where you had to pay for it.

Court mourning for the late King George came to an end on July 20. We all knew it couldn't be long now till King

Edward would come visiting. But there were various matters postponed during the mourning period, that had first to be attended to, such as presentations of the debutantes. "Jesus Bloody Hurrah. The country sinking, but them fancy bitches got to curtsey to the King. What do they mean by 'Coming Out'? I bet a quid he is as fed up at such rot as me." My father knocked back half a bottle of his "comforter" at these delays.

My mother cried, "Good Gracious me! You drink the stuff like milk. Shall I put it in a baby's bottle for you with a rubber tit?"

He started his fifth refill when he learned that the King would be gone out of the country for the entire month of August. His Majesty was going on a Mediterranean – Adriatic cruise in a chartered yacht called Nahlin. Not that my father begrudged the King his holiday and happiness, but the strain of waiting had begun to tell. He was like an elastic rubberband turned white from stretching to the snapping point. He had bad dreams.

One night I woke to hear a horrible demented raving coming from my parents' room. When I rushed along to check, my father was sitting up in bed, his face grey, his hair on end. My mother stood behind the footrail of the bedstead. She was clutching the smocked neckline of her summer cotton tent, her curlers loose, her net awry.

"Chrissake, what happened?" said my father.

"You had me by the throat, about to do me in!" my mother croaked, pounding on her chest to still her heart or knock it back in place.

"Gorstruth, I'm sorry, Gladys, love. But I had a nightmare. There was this crowd of ugly black-robed men. They were hounding the King with crooks and nets and stones. Herding him towards a precipice. I leapt at one big bastard and got him round the throat – "

"*My* throat!" my mother snapped, returning to the bed-head. Gingerly fingering her windpipe, she winced elaborately. "It must be your malaria," which he'd contracted in the war. "Indeed I see your pillow's soaking wet. Viddy, run and fetch him his quinine."

At that time, the meaning of the dream seemed obvious. I privately interpreted it as reluctance on my father's part to carry out the awesome plan to buttonhole the King. He'd be bound to have these hidden qualms despite his certainty of its necessity. A few months later I was to wonder if that nightmare wasn't prescient of something else entirely.

The King returned to England in the middle of September. He spent two weeks at Balmoral in the Scottish Highlands before taking up official residence in Buckingham Palace. Queen Mary had only recently moved out – we wondered why. With all that room.

Then came the cockle-warming news to prove my father's second sight. The Autumn Calendar was published, listing duties and appearances making up the royal round. A visit to the South Wales coalfield was included there as plain as day. No dates or details yet, of course. But no doubt about it. He was "Coming Soon". My father's mumpy would at last be realized.

But instead of being jubilant, he became quiet and introverted. Knowing his secret, but unable to share it, I fell into anxiety. The tension grew unbearable.

CHAPTER 13
SEPTEMBER TO OCTOBER, 1936

My sister Muriel's employers retired to Nassau that September. She came home to live for good. My mother finagled her a serving job in Pattimore's Caernarvon Stores. She would work at first for nothing, to pay off our accumulated grocery debts. If she proved a glutton for the work, she would graduate to seven-and-six a week. There'd be occasional bonuses; perhaps a crushed box of cracker biscuits, some butter likely to turn rancid, or a rasher or two of dried-out streaky bacon on which the salt had crystallized.

Pretty, sweet and seventeen was an explosive combination. With Nancy Turner gone and Angelo on the loose again, it was imperative to find a nice young man to take her off my hands as fast as possible.

More easily thought than done, however. It had to be a chap a cut above the mill hands down the works. Somebody who cleaned his teeth and cut his nails and was not averse to soap and water now and then. On the other hand, neither would a dainty type like Ronald Penrick fit the bill. My father reckoned he had crochet edging on his singlet and his underpants.

Manly and moral was only the half of it. The fellow had to be good-looking, too. There was not much chance I could come up with any handsome Latin specimen. Some of our Welsh boys did look rather foreign, as though they might be sired by shoni-onion men from Brittany. Others looked like throwbacks to Bronze Age Iberians, who were reputed to have settled Wales before the Celts. Unfortunately, the chaps who had the colouring of such ancient ancestry were inclined to have their caveman looks besides.

I was still looking for this Galahad when Roasting Guyer Night came around. The name is our mangled version of the Welsh *Nos cyn Gaeaf*, "the Night Before Winter" – a cross between that ancient folk custom when the sheep were brought down from the mountain, and the Christian All Saints or Hallowe'en. Our gang was up the back lane, roasting spuds and onions and telling ghost stories around a fire, when Ruby Jones came hunting me. "Did you see Tich?" she said.

"No, why?"

"I thought he might have told you he was going."

"Going where?" I said.

She fidgeted from one foot to the other, reluctant to express herself.

I said, "Be quick and out with it"

"I saw him at the second lock." Ruby often went off alone to fret and moon. She had done so since her father's death. "Tich said your Muriel was off to meet Ben Lanzo's cousin at the bridge."

"Cor damn! The little bitch. You can't trust her any better than the cat."

From Ruby's information, I quickly calculated the head start they must have had. I ran until my legs were rubber and my chest caught fire. All the while my brain was churning. Should I fork off up the mountain fields or gamble on the second bank? A thick mist drifted down the mountain. It would soon blot out the moon and stars.

I had started to despair of finding them when I saw Tich Veasey skulking in the bushes on the verge ahead. I assumed he'd stopped there to relieve himself. But before I hailed him, I noticed he was jiggling round and craning through the hedge.

I decided to creep up on him. He didn't hear me, he was so engrossed. I made out, through the gloom, the cuddling couple he was spying on beyond the gate. They were still standing on their feet, thank all the hallowed saints who fight the demons on this night.

I backed up twenty or more paces, Tich none the wiser. I started calling softly, "Our Mu, where are you?" repeating it and gradually increasing the volume of my voice as I advanced. Old Tich whirled, petrified. I said, "Oh, hullo, Tich. You been here long? Seen our Mu around here any-where?"

He gesticulated wildly, mutely, to shut me up, and pointed to the gate. I pretended to be dull and boomed with thespian surprise, "You mean she's gone into that field? Whatever for?"

The shadowy outline of the clinching couple disappeared.

Tich put his fists up to his head in a gesture of excruciating agony. Making my voice stern, I said, "Don't tell me she is with a chap! Who the hell – ?"

That flushed her out. She was through the gate before I had taken two steps forward. "Thank God," I sighed. "Our Mam has called in the police to search for you. She is in a bloody state. You had better hoof it home in double time."

No more was said. Tich cringed. Angelo stayed hidden. My sister fell in step with me.

Well out of earshot of the other two and close to home, I said. "You will want to knock me clear into next week for this. But it was only for your own good. No bobbies are out looking. Our Mam don't even know you're gone – "

"Why, you mischievous little devil." She went for me like a cornered rat.

"Whoa, whoa, there," I said, ducking her flaying arms. "I know who you were with. You're mad at me right now. But one day you will thank your blessed stars for what I saved

you from. That fellow's eaten up with some disease. The
rumour is around the village that Nance Turner caught it
from him and is gone away to get a cure. Besides, what with
the rotten turn he served her, I would have thought you
would think better about keeping company with such a sod."

The morals of the fellow didn't seem to bother her as
much as did the reference to disease. She cross-examined
me. At that time I was pretty ignorant of sexual pathology.
It was my good fortune she was dumb and gullible. I liberally
adapted what I knew of Bible leprosy. I remembered the
theme I had used in my anonymous letter, and pointed out
the damage it would do her reputation.

She said, "If I find out you are lying, you are not long for
this world."

But at least while she was finding out, the inhibition
worked. And in the buffer period, relief was sighted. Not
two days later, Nick Vowles the Baker brought Leonard
Hasty to our house to join the Loyal Order of the Prince of
Wales.

A most presentable young man was Leonard. A railway
clerk. Good, steady work. His noble profile suggested that
way back in his ancestry, first century AD, a Roman
legionary may have courted a Silurian maid of this locality.
Before Leonard left our house that evening, he and our
Muriel had formed a Loyal Order of their own. Before the
weekend, she had started walking out with him. I could
only keep my fingers crossed.

CHAPTER 14
NOVEMBER, 1936

My father's rabid combing of the papers was rewarded, at the beginning of November, with the first sketchy mention of the King's upcoming tour. There were still no details to help the Loyal Order plan their secret manoeuvures.

There was plenty in the news to dispel any lingering doubts about going through with their intent. Two hundred Jarrow residents had marched to London from the depressed area of Tyneside to talk to the Prime Minister. They wanted to object to the Iron and Steel Federation's failure to erect a new works in their town. But when the marchers reached the capital, the Prime Minister refused to see them.

"Ours is the only way to get a hearing," said Ted Swilling.

"Watch it, mun!" my father growled, darting a warning glance in my direction. I quickly donned my look of meek and mild.

The King made his first Speech to Parliament on November 3. The Government programme he was forced to parrot was a patchy, piecemeal farce. "Fiddling while Rome burns," my father scoffed.

Pulling in her double chin pouter-pigeon fashion, my mother said, "What price your precious King, now, is it?"

My father eyed her, open-mouthed, then cast heavenwards a supplicating glance. I grinned; he winked. With the tenderness he always showed to innocence, he said, "The speech don't show his own convictions, love. He only reads out what the Government do tell him to. If it was left to him,

he'd overhaul this nation's industry from top to bottom."
He vigorously flicked his tongue around his teeth, a sure
sign that he was ruminating. "I wager that them rotters are
quaking in their shoes at what he's going to see and say
down here. They couldn't stop him coming, but sure as eggs
they'll try and put the bit and blinkers on him." He split a
matchstick with his teeth to toothpick size. "But us'll put a –"
He broke off in the nick of time.

He gave me a sharp look. I attempted to look blank. I
might have played a shade too innocent.

More to throw him off than anything, I said, "It's a scandal,
en it, them putting up the ministers' salaries. I mean, if I
was an MP, I wouldn't have the cheek to give myself a rise,
when half of us down here are on the dole or poor relief."

I was coming up fourteen, and there wasn't much got by
me. I read everything I got my hands on and had a good
grasp of the issues. But I didn't very often vent my own
opinions, except in question form.

"Oh, thinking of putting up for the Government, now, is
it?" said my mother, heavily sardonic. "Don't have a penny
in your pocket but aim to be a toff."

"Oh, come on, Glad. They ent all toffs in Parliament. Take
Nye Bevan. There'd be plenty more like us up there, if all
them stupid buggers who put the Conservatives in voted
the way their bread was buttered."

"That's right! Encourage her! She should be thinking how
to make her living, not talking politics." She snatched the
butterdish away as though to say I'd have to earn it if I
wanted any more.

These little scuffles about my future, with my father egging
me on to follow my ideals and my mother tugging me back
to focus on pounds, shillings and pence, helped me define
myself. Whether politics was in my nature, or whether I was
nurtured into it, didn't really matter. It was in my marrow.

By now my father and his butties were such open books, I knew all their reactions to the Government proposals almost before they knew themselves. Take the one about rearmament. Obie would be worried about what it was the Government must know (that we didn't) about possible aggression. Unbeknowns to us, Germany was colluding with Japan and Italy, with World War II less than three years away. We had only the dimmest notion of how things lay. Obie would join my father in realizing that rearmament at least meant the prospect of more jobs. But they would both readily agree with Nwd there was a darker side to that: What was the point of improved employment making weapons, if they and their sons would end up manning them?

Pacifist Twm Sion Gruffydd was appalled, and Emrys furious, at "this capitalist warmongering". It was nothing but a ruse to take up economic slack and line the pockets of munitions profiteers. On the other hand, a jeering Angelo sneered that it betrayed fright at the growing might of Italy and Germany.

Emrys and Angelo were jointly livid at the stated intention of the Government to curb "the fascist and communist menace to public order." When a bill was read in Parliament the following week prohibiting Sir Oswald Moseley's British Fascists from wearing their black shirts, it fanned the common cause of those strange bedfellows.

There was, in my father's view, only one good thing to be said about the opening of Parliament. That was the King's rejection of the customary folderol of gilded coach and horses in favour of a modern motor car.

With the King's tour scheduled, I had to keep abreast of what was going on. To make time, I grappled with homework on train rides to and back from school. While the other kids swung from the luggage racks or reclined in them like hammocks, copped puffs of cigs, huffed on the carriage mirror to play noughts and crosses in their breath, bounded on the seats beating out the acrid dust, leaned halfway out of windows to spit into the wind and duck back in so it flew into a neighbour's face, jeered at the older girls vainly struggling to look beautiful in thick black stockings and basin hats, I skipped that fun for a far more stimulating, thrilling kind in my freed evenings.

"Where are you off to now, our Vid?"

"Down Bryns's to help him work a theorem, Our Mam." Or, "Ruby's having trouble with her Latin, look." By playing on her pride at having a daughter brainy enough to teach her peers, I blunted her suspicions. I was free to cruise the back lane gleaning odd information where I could.

On November 4, the tempo picked up noticeably. My father's butties scurried back and forth like harriers, buzzing over minor changes which the *Argus* had reported. The King would stop off at the cenotaph in Blaenavon to lay a wreath. Was that to be their opportunity?

The next night there was even more activity. Not just because it happened to be Bonfire Night. I remember, remember that Fifth of November not for Guy Fawkes's "gunpowder, treason and plot" to blow up Parliament three centuries ago, but for the plot being cooked up by my father and his co-conspirators. While my father helped us dress the scarecrow of the guy and pile the brush and kindling ten feet high upon the pyre, as he had done every year I could remember, he continued hurried, intense exchanges with Ted Swilling, Bryn Thomas's father, Idris, Mr. Chesterton, and other members of the Loyal Order resident in Panty-gasseg Place. Their excitement crackled louder than the bonfire.

For that evening's *Argus* had reported that the King had now approved in general outline his South Wales itinerary.

Wednesday, November 18, a bare two weeks away, he would start at Llantwit Major and end the day at Penrhiwceibr. That much had been expected. The Glamorgan valleys always bellyached the loudest, and got paid the most attention.

But the bit that made the spirits soar was the programme for the following day. Starting at Llantarnum, he would tour *our* valley. Llantarnum was only a tupny or thrupny bus-ride down the road!

It was as though the King was meant to set foot in our district so his devotees could have their little chat with him. It made them feel the Chosen, the Elect. It put the stamp of Destiny upon the enterprise.

I personally was more alarmed than thrilled. I hoped to God it wouldn't be my old man whom the kids three centuries ahead would burn in effigy in bonfires on a million back lanes. My flesh goosed to imagine twenty-third century brats going house to house begging pennies for a guy named Fred E. Williams whose plot to accost King Edward VIII had been foiled in the nick of time. I was even more terrified to think what would become of him right on the spot. Did they still behead the perpetrators of lese-majesty in London Tower? Or deport them down under like John Frost, the rebel Chartist leader, when last century he stormed the Westgate Hotel in Newport, for the same cause as my father: justice for the common man? Or would they hang him by the neck till dead in Monmouth Gaol?

Next day, November 6, after a restless night, I got up early. My father was on nights that week. When he was on that shift, he arrived home shortly after 6 am. He'd treat my mother to a long lie-in, while he helped to get me off to school. He made delicious lunchbox sandwiches. My mother hacked the loaf to death in crumbly, scooping hunks, while he cut his slices flat and wafer thin. He was also generous with the butter; no bread-and-scrape for him.

When I went into the kitchen, he stood gazing down on a rosy fire and the purring kettle on the trivet. I saw that he was folding up a sheet of paper rather small. At sight of me, he jumped a guilty mile. I saw him drop the wadded paper on the floor and quickly stamp his boot on it. While I fumbled in the slipper box for socks, pretending to be unaware, I saw him swiftly pick it up and stuff it down behind the cushion of his chair.

I guessed that it might be a dirty joke or picture, something he considered too salty to share with me. Later, when he went out, down the baily, I pounced on it.

Indecent, coarse, it was all right. But in another kind of way. Printed on the paper were several scurrilous bits about the King. Words like "fast", "fashionable" and "sophisticated international set" jumped out. Charges about cocktail glasses set on secret documents with German Generals present. Innuendoes about blind eyes turned towards Mussolini's muscling in on little helpless nations. Snide remarks expressed as questions about King Edward's "interest" in Nazism. Hints of gorgeous mataharis, and the like.

The boldest insinuations were that the King was carrying on with a fancy woman from America. It had been going on for years, it said, even though she had a husband. The lady had applied for a divorce at the Ipswich Assizes. She'd just been granted a decree nisi, whatever that might mean. A verbatim newspaper quotation followed: "New York Journal American, October 26, 1936. In all human probability, in June 1937, one month after the ceremonies of the Coronation, will follow the festivities of the marriage of King Edward VIII to the very charming and intelligent Mrs. Ernest Simpson of Baltimore, Maryland, U.S.A."

I was so absorbed, I failed to keep my wits about me. I didn't hear the chain pull. Suddenly, my father stood in front of me. He glowered as if to strike me dead.

The next minute, the furrows flattened, and he chucked his head resignedly, "Well, there you are!"

Feeling pretty cheap, I said, "I'm sorry, our Dad."

"You are a nibs. You saw me put it there."

"Aye."

He shook his head and smiled a grudging grin. "There ent much misses you, mind, is it?"

"Not much."

Narrowing his eyes at me, he said, "I suppose you know the rest, too, then. It have occurred to me to wonder."

Fearing to implicate myself unnecessarily, I held my peace.

He prompted, "About the Loyal Order plans regards the King."

I reluctantly owned up, "A little bit."

He sighed. "I should have known. You are such a quiet *swch*. See all, say nowt. Deep as a draw well. When it boils right down, I suppose it is a talent that will stand you in good stead. I am to blame not bearing it in mind how keen you are. But listen here, my girl. You breathe a single word to anybody, and I'll have your bleeding block off." Softly, parenthetically, "Or they'll have mine."

"Aye, mun. I understand."

He put the folded paper in his inside pocket. He took the teapot off the hob and poured himself a treacly-looking cup. Then he laid the cloth halfway across the table, fetched the bread and butter from the pantry, a jar of bloater paste, a pot of lemon curd, and started on my sandwiches.

While I buffed my toes, I dared to ask, "Our Dad, about them cuttings. Are they true?"

"Filthy bloody rumours to blacken his good name."

"Who gave it you?"

"Emrys, naturally. Bolshie skulduggery. Always stirring up the mud. Might be it came from Angelo."

"Do you think there's something in it?"

"The German bit?" He shrugged. "Any programmes to solve social problems interest him. But that ent agreement, is it?"

"I mean the woman."

He pondered while he operated like a French chef on the elegant sandwiches. At last he said, "I think a king should marry who he please, like any other man. We ent living in the bloody Middle Ages. Besides, America don't have no royalty, yet they are getting to be mightier than France or Germany. Not only that, Americans be more our sort of people than any of them European royalty. They speak our tongue. It is a country of the common man."

He put the greaseproof package in my satchel with a russet apple from my Granddad's tree. "So if there is a grain of truth in it, it ent of any consequence to me. King Ted should ought to have the girl he wants. Good luck to him. He've waited long enough."

But what I'd read stayed with me, like a worry. Or a threat.

CHAPTER 15
NOVEMBER 13, 1936

With the King's visit looming, it was all to the good my father had found me out. I could engineer my inclusion in the intrigue by making myself indispensable. My father benefited by having a bosom-of-the-family confidante, as well as an extra pair of legs and a spare thinking box. I fetched and carried messages with maximum discretion and reliability. I made circumspect suggestions, some of which were seized upon as nothing short of brilliant. One was that Obie put a bid in early with Bob Miller, Chairman of the Urban Council, to have the Loyal Order serve as Honour Guard for His Majesty. This would give them cover for their secret operations, as well as a key position to effect the intended rendezvous. Obie happened to be in like Flynn with Bob for using his considerable influence to swing Union votes to Bob's support. He was granted the provisional favour like a flash.

Being "in" did not automatically entitle me to their full confidence, of course. But with my sensitive antennae, information wasn't hard to come by now they weren't on guard with me.

Day by day the tension mounted. On the 12th, the evening's *Argus* contained the official timetable. The Big Event was just six days away. Listen to this: the royal train would stop at *our own* station at 9.30 in the morning. And Hallelujah, the King was going to get off.

Just think of it. The King was going to get off and tread the ground we regularly trod. You almost felt it was a consecration of our local native soil.

Sir Kingsley Wood, the account continued, would present the Chairman and Clerk of the Urban District Council, and His Majesty would then continue on by road. He would arrive then at Llanfrechfa at 9.50 am, where Mr. Ernest Brown would present the wardens. At that speed, a fat lot of sight we'd have of him.

I went to bed as usual. But I got under the bed clothes fully dressed. With time so short, they would have to draft the details of the plot post-haste to leave sufficient time for preparation. With work finished for the week, I wagered they would meet that night.

My father came in off the two-till-ten shift only slightly later than his normal time. He was unusually taciturn. I guessed that he re-read the *Argus* while he ate his fish and chips. I strained my ears for full reception.

At last his voice rose up the chimney. "I have got to go back down the club tonight a bit, Glad. You go on up to bed."

"Down the club? Tonight? Whatever for?"

"Planning and rehearsal of the Honour Guard."

"To guzzle beer more like it."

Heavily patient, he sighed, "You will notice it is gone closing time. If it was booze I'd wanted, I would have popped in coming home. With us working all next week, we have got to make the most of this weekend. It's the only way to put our best foot forward." His tone changed. He said peevishly, "All these months we've been on short time. Then just when we could do with some time off, work have brightened up a bit. En fate contrary!"

"Don't flout it," snapped my mother. "Be glad with Christmas coming on."

I couldn't miss that meeting for all the sheep upon the mountain nor all the coal below. After my father clicked the latch and clomped along the yard, I listened for my mother to retire. She put the dishes in the bosh, banked and put the guard around the fire and shot the bolt on the front door. Luckily she must have put her curlers in before my father came, for in another couple of seconds I heard her steps along the landing. The door of the big bedroom closed with its customary little whoosh.

I was out of bed in bullet time. I took care not to lean against the banister and make it groan, or bump my heels against the carpet rods and clang them in their sockets, or tread too heavily on the creaky-turn-the-corner step. In a jiffy I was out of the backdoor, through the garden gate without a mishap, flying like the wind past Poulton's garden.

I caught up with my father outside Gus Black-the-undertaker's barn.

"Go on home and back to bed at once," he tried to thunder in a whisper.

"Aw, come on, our Dad. You need me to stand guard."

He pulled his nostrils. "If you're so cunning you know everything that's going on, I can't see how we'd do without you. I suppose we'll need a look-out, yes. All right. Come on."

There was no describing the excitement in the back room of the Legion that momentous night. It was not the sparkly effervescence of a glass of Enos fruit salts but the corked variety. It was like when Idris bottled up a batch of stout before the barm stopped working, and the flagons burst all over his aunt's pantry floor.

My father's fierce abhorrence of anything that smacked of an elite or clique had set him stubbornly against the idea of a subcommittee to draft the final plans. However unwieldy and long-winded, he insisted that the action should be thrashed out on the floor.

By rough count, a good three quarters of the roll were present, the absentees presumably on nights. Those who had come from work were in dark, shabby oddments of old suits, their flannel sweatshirts underneath, their faces stubbled. Those off earlier shifts sported second-best serge suits and shaven chins, shirt collars turned, the cuffs fray-trimmed.

Instead of sitting in regular meeting style on straight-back, front-facing chairs, they squatted cross-legged in a plotting circle on the floor. The single gas jet had been turned so low that it burned a ghostly blue. It flickered ominously on occasion as if another shilling would be needed in the meter any minute.

Bear in mind that until that moment when my father called the membership to order, we all had only the vaguest thoughts about how this latest facet of his mumpy was going to shape up. We all appreciated that the general aim was somehow to take the King aside and appeal to him as man to man for help in our predicament. But there had been little talk about preliminary specifics, let alone any precise, detailed discussion about how to bell the cat.

Everybody knew by now the perils of their plan. To approach the King would be construed by established authority as a threat to the health and safety of the sovereign. Up to now many members had successfully suppressed their trepidation with the thought that it might never happen.

But there was no longer any ducking it. At last we were right up against the scratch line. Within minutes of my father calling the floor to order, everyone was using words like "nab", "grab", "snatch", and "bag". It was clear they knew exactly what they had to do to reach their King. In short, the mumpy's final form could only be defined as King-napping.

My heart was in my throat now. Despite the risky nature of the act ahead, no one stopped to offer second thoughts. Unanimous agreement was reached without the need for words. Fate had sealed their mission by bringing the King to our home territory. Lifelong familiarity with every nook and inch of it, plus the Loyal Order's inclusion in the Honour Guard, gave them extraordinary tactical advantages. If they refused this chance, indelible regret would be the consequence.

The only things left to be discussed were exactly where and how.

"If He comes from Pontypool, He'll alight the downside and have to come across the line," said Idris. By unprecedented aspiration of his aitches, he reverently capitalized each He and Him and His when referring to the King. "We could nab Him on the bridge. Edge Him off onto some goods train standing underneath."

"Have a bit of sense, mun. That would break His bleeding neck," Ted Swilling said.

Leonard Hasty, our Muriel's new bloke, a railway clerk, said, "Besides, the lines will all be clear. They'll stop the regular runs."

My father said, "Before going off half-cocked, let's hear from you, Obe. What did you find out from Bob Miller?"

"The people let on the platform for the introductions will be strictly limited. So Bob would like the Honour Guard to line the route between the station exit and down to where the road widens and forks off. That's where they'll need us most, to hold the crowds in check. If we keep it mum, he said, he'll give us first choice of our ten-yard stretch."

Uncle Jack said, "The best thing then would be to pick a shop to snatch Him into. Harrison's Greengrocers, say."

"Evans the Confectioner is very sympathetic," Nick Vowles volunteered.

"Naih, mun, won't work," said Barney. "He'll be walking down the middle of the road not on the pavement. Like a bride going down the aisle. Nowhere we can pull him into there."

The general sag in spirits was like a tyre puncturing.

An anxious silence was broken by a cautious, hesitating comment from my father, "The street ent quite *that* empty in the middle, is it? You can't say there's *nothing* there." He rubbed his scratchy chin, reflecting.

Another pause, but pregnant now.

"I mean," my father said, "what about the gentlemen's convenience?"

I sucked in my breath. Centrally located, smack in the middle of a very wide place at the fork, sat an ancient urinal. It was flanked on the far side by the Police Station, several shops and Vowles's Bakery. On the side where the road diverged towards Newport there were more shops, the Pantheon Cinema, and the Old Crown pub. This convenience was a sheet metal circular arrangement with a wrought iron dome. It covered an area maybe twelve feet in diameter, and stood roughly eight or nine feet high. I was ignorant of its interior, having never been invited in to look. The whole thing was a bilious dark green, the hue my father called shwt-colour-drab. It had a lamp on top.

His suggestion went down like a water-logged boiled suet pudding. Nwd gently chided, "It wouldn't be quite right, look, would it, Fred? To take His Majesty in there."

Perce Cook said, "Stinks to high heaven. Knock you over quicker than a whiff of poison gas at Mons."

They all shook their heads regretfully and made various clicking noises with their tongues.

But Ted Swilling chewed his cheeks as though reflecting. He said uncertainly, "It would have to be a last resort."

Then Bryn Thomas's father muttered, "Beggars can't be choosers, though. Maybe it ent a bad idea at that."

Said Mr. Chesterton, "If the place is so unlikely, that *could* be in its favour. Nobody would dream He'd be in such a place."

Twm Sion Gruffydd's mouth worked like an old woman reckoning her change. Being a sanitary engineer, he commanded full attention when he suddenly burst out, "Caustic soda, scrub it down and flush it out. It would smell as sweet as violets after I got done with it." His mouth began to tremble and his black eyes shone. "Duw, Duw, it comes to me this is my reason, look, for being here. It is written in my destiny to do this thing. My blood is telling me that this here public lavatory was *meant* to be our place of assignation with our King." For somebody as Baptist as he was supposed to be, he sounded dangerously pagan. "My sixth sense and my second sight are telling me I am to tinker with the plumbing. Put it out of order for a day or two. They will have to shut it up and send for me to mend it, giving me the key. Unfortunately, I shall be held up for a day or two getting the proper piece of pipe I need . . ."

"For a Chapel Christian, you sure be bloody crafty, mun," Tich Veasey's father said admiringly.

Twm Sion retorted, "It is a noble worthwhile cause I do it in. The end do justify the means."

My father was elated. "And after you have cleaned it, Twm, we'll deck it out fit for a king. If an 'oman can make a home out of a hovel, we ought to be able to make a palace out of a lavatory." He used the euphemism to suit the royal context. He had several synonyms available.

The plotters roared delightedly.

Emrys challenged, "Deck it out? What with, Fred?"

"What with do you think? Anything pretty. A bit of lace and plush, feathers and ribbons. A couple of pictures hanging on the walls."

"Where in the bloody world – ?" said Emrys.

Barney interrupted, "Mother of God. If Twm Sion the Plumber has got a destiny for being here, then so has a poor rag-and-bone man like myself. I shall make a special trip around the swanky houses. Rustle up some finery." His face shone.

An excited buzz ran through the room.

They would have dawdled over the pleasant details of interior decoration of the urinal. But Obie reined them back on track. "Even if we settle on the Gents' Convenience, how'll we get Him into it?"

Ted said, "That's easy, Obe. Ask Bob Miller to assign us the ten yards before the Gents. The King is only Fred's size here. We'll close around Him and nudge Him through the door."

"We shall have to see our bloody hands are lily white to touch His Royal Personage."

"What if He lets out a squawk?" This from Tich Veasey's father, gleeful at the mere thought.

"Christ, mate, a King is too refined to squawk," said Uncle Bill.

"And if He do," said Gib, "the massed bands will be blowing out their flippin' lungs. And everybody will be cheering their blinkin' heads off."

"All eyes, however, will be on Him," said Ruby Jones's uncle. "If He should scuffle . . ."

"Now there's a snag," my father said.

And Obie added, "And here's another bridge to cross; Ernie Brown, Sir Kingsley Wood and His special constable will have to be distracted at the crucial minute."

"The question's how." My father frowned.

Uncle Bill said, "Remember that there ruckus in the summer? When that chap McMahon flung the loaded gun into the road in front of the King's horse? Couldn't we wangle a similar commotion? Like shoot a gun into the air?"

"By George," my father cried. "Someone on a roof creating a disturbance. *Everyone* would look away."

Obie said, "That would be a nasty job to ask of anybody, mun. Who did it would be seen and caught."

"McMahon only got a year's hard labour."

"Only because the jury felt he wasn't quite all there."

Suddenly everyone was scrutinizing everybody else, their eyes inquiring, Who among us is so nutty he could get off easy if he happened to get caught?

In a funny voice, Perce Cook said, "Where is Clarence, then?"

My father answered sheepishly, "I thought it better not to mention we were meeting. In case he should forget himself and let rip round the village."

"Shouting from the rooftops is right up his street. It would be natural. The police wouldn't even take him in. And even if he was had on, no jury would go hard."

There was a cogitating silence. You could hear the gas jet sputter.

Bryn Thomas's father said, "So will you ask him, Fred?"

My father nodded. "He'll be glad to do his bit, I'll back."

There was a hub-bub of relief, a lighting up of smokes. All the big questions were left hanging.

Obie said, "I hate to think up all these hurdles. But before we take it any further, how'll we manage if the King should happen not to walk – if he's riding in a motor car?"

"You can fix that with Bob Miller, can't you, Obe? Point out to him the little kids won't get a look in if He doesn't walk. Bob is very sentimental about the kiddies; he'll turn somersaults for them."

Perce Cook said, "Even if He rides, the car will crawl at snail's pace through the crowd. We'd naturally close ranks around the car to guard the King from raving lunatics up on the roof." It was like making up a picture for the cinema.

"With his driver flustered, trying not to run us over . . ."

"And the others distracted . . ."

There were claps and nods of general assent.

Obie said, "And when we've got Him in the Gents, what then?"

Idris said, "Make Him feel at home, mun. Show Him to a chair. P'raps offer Him a cup of tea." When the laughter died down, Idris protested, "No, mun, I'm serious. I could fetch my little oil stove that I use when we go rabbiting out Usk. Else bring a thermos flask. There is nothing like a cuppa cha to give you confidence and put a soul at ease. Naturally His Majesty will be a wee bit startled. We have got to reassure Him ready for our Little Chat."

Obie said, "I'm very much afraid there won't be time for that. Have any of you thought that He'll be missed at once? We can't kidnap his whole entourage. In an instant they'll be crying foul. They'll go over the entire area with a fine tooth comb. They're bound to search the Gents. They'll cook our goose before we've even had a chance to speak to Him."

Nwd said thoughtfully, "What is called for is a secret tunnel, p'raps. That is where *I* could come in." In his teenage collier days, before they closed his pit, he had been a champion at tunnelling and propping, even winning timbering competitions in Brynmawr.

"Over to our bakery, maybe," Nick Vowles supplied.

"Or ent there a branch sewer underneath it, Twm?" said Uncle Bill.

Emrys, who had kept himself aloof for most of the meeting, was leering scornfully from the sidelines. I, too, felt it was all a bit much. They seemed carried away by a creative surge. It was more fun making up stories than keeping a rational eye on the main business.

Obie pulled them gently out of this preposterous sidetrack. "If they're on the warpath, there is nothing they won't find. It won't be only Sergeant Rodney and old P.C. Wiley doddering around. The Monmouthshire Constabulary will be out in full force, you can bank on that. It seems to me our plot is doomed unless they're kept in blissful ignorance a little while. Not realise he's gone."

Nwd shook his head. "That is a stile it is impossible to jump."

Everyone looked pained and glum.

Well, not quite everybody. Looking as though he'd found a pound note lying in the road my father said, "Never say die. There is one way we can breast this little obstacle." When they all looked mystified, he laughed, "I am very disappointed in the lot of you. Have you had me on for all these years?"

When they still looked blank, he grew genuinely huffy. "Jesus gi'me strength. Who have you always said I looked the spitting image of?"

A gasp went up. Surprise and more than that.

Ted Swilling croaked, "Name of God. You wouldn't dare."

"Why not? We're already daring all we've got," my father said. "Is it any worse than asking Clarence to shout bloody murder from the roof? I'd count it a great privilege to take His place a little while and damn the risks. If we're caught, it won't go any harder on Fred Williams because he posed as King of England for a couple of minutes."

"Like Him you may be, Fred. But not that like."

"Hell, there's enough resemblance to keep it going for a bit. I'll sneeze and cough into my hankie. Sit hunched up in the corner of the car. I'll be turned away from the others, looking out the window. The crowds only ever get a fleeting glimpse as He drives by. Nobody would be the wiser that I wasn't Him."

Cautiously they tried on the suggestion. It didn't take much getting used to. Soon they were granting that it might be workable. A few more minutes, and they were congratulating one another on their cleverness. They couldn't have been more pleased if they had won a raffle or a sweepstake.

But what they regarded as a stroke of luck, my father no doubt was construing as a revelation of his life's purpose.

His resemblance to King Edward could never more be viewed as mere coincidence. The psychic bond was real. It was ordained, if not by Divine Will, then by the secular equivalent, for him to be a stand-in for the King.

For the substitution to succeed, however, many details needed solving. What would the King be wearing? Some top brass uniforms would be impossible to duplicate. But the King would more than likely wear his usual – his "uniform of the common man", a plain topcoat and bowler hat. My father said, "A bowler is a bowler any way you look at it. So's a man's topcoat, except for colour. Though it is certain to be black or grey. The answer is to have several on hand. Find out what he's wearing the first day of the tour."

Leonard Hasty said, "I can verify it on the morning of the day itself, by telegraphing Usk. That's where the King will spend the night. The rumour is they'll shunt the Royal Train into a siding there."

Obie said, "How long, Fred, do you think you'd get away with it?" Obie was never very certain about anything.

"I dare say I could make it to Llanfrechfa. I'm afraid that would be it. Fool them with my looks while huddled in the car, I might. But not close up. Not with my ignorant old talk. I doubt I could put on an Oxford accent. I'm likely to forget and cuss. Besides, look at my bloody hands." He viewed them ruefully. "Horny as bleeding toads. They'd know as soon as I shook hands they were no gentleman's."

"What'll happen to you then, Fred?" said my Uncle Jack.

"I will count on you to fetch Him to Llanfrechfa and make the swap back at the Grange. We'll have to play that bit by ear. By that time we should have Him on our side. Then it wouldn't matter if it all came out. The King will see that we get lenience. If we get that far, the rest can look after itself."

Nwd said, "According to the schedule, there'll be less than twenty minutes to do our talking and catch up with you."

Angelo made up for his long silence with a flash of inspiration to overcome that hurdle. "Kill two birds with one stone," he said. "Back a van up to the latrine door, whip Him into it, detour up around the left-hand fork to miss the snarl. Join on the rear of the caravan of cars driving to the Grange. Say our piece to Him as we are driving over."

"You've got a head on you!"

"There's brains!"

And then, "Whose van?"

Nick Vowles nodded gladly when they looked his way. He would be honoured. "I always keep it nice," he said. "But I'll see it gets an extra polish for the Day. A lovely yeasty smell as well it has. Be nice for Him."

Barney O'Quirk said, "We can decorate it up the same as the convenience. Put cushions on the racks for him to perch on. Maybe a comfy chair."

"You'll drive it careful, Nick," said Mr. Chesterton.

Nick pulled back. "Me drive? Oh, no. I wouldn't dream. I dursn't, knowing whose dear life depended on it."

When it boiled right down, there weren't but two or three of the entire membership who had ever been behind a wheel. Driving was for better-offs and trade. Mr. MacDour in his capacity as travelling draper to outlying areas, drove a motor-bike-and-sidecar to transport his wares. But he begged off on similar grounds. The others in business on their own account, Barney and Gib the Milk, drove horse and cart.

Only Angelo, with his experience on a biscuit lorry, had both the skill and confidence to mesh those gears and steer that wheel for such a precious cargo. Nick Vowles agreed to give him a few practice runs.

"So all that's left for us to settle is what we're going to say to Him when we've got Him in the van," my father said. "We'll have to talk fast, 'on't us? Only fifteen minutes to say everything." He blew hard up his face as if sweltering from the rush of it.

"Fred?" said Obie softly, as though awakening him. "Did you forget? *You* won't be the one to talk to Him. You can't be in two places at one time."

"Oh, bust," my father blurted like a disappointed child. You could see him wrestling with the painful irony. To be so close to his life's ambition to twin up with Him, yet fail to do it.

But he rose to the occasion like the trump he was. "Well, there it is. I shall have to make that sacrifice." Moreover, he saw very clearly that for speed and comfort only one comrade should parley with the King. "It would have to be you, Obe, at any rate. You are a better talker by a long shot than any of the rest of us."

As a sort of consolation afterthought, he said, "Though once you've won His confidence, p'raps you could persuade Him to sit down around a table with us all. I'd like to meet Him, shake His hand." Smiling wistfully, he finished, "We'll be counting on you, Obe, to appeal to all that's warm and grand in Him. He'll understand."

It was the wee small hours when they finally broke up. Going home, my father said to me, "Marvelous how everything fell into place. It worked out beautiful."

"Like clockwork," I agreed. But I was far from confidant about it all. "Oh, ye of little faith" was frequently applied to me by my mother and her like. I was already on the stony road of doubt and cynicism, with a taste for negative, ironic aphorisms: Hope is a swindle. Reason's a rare breed. You can't change anybody's mind, especially an enthusiast's. Death and debt are the only certainties.

My father said, "If there is such a thing as Fate, Vid, it is with us this night. I feel it in my bones."

This surprised me. Some of my attitude of scepticism came from him. But he was talking like the rest of them who felt privileged to be a pawn in Fortune's game – as though that had more merit than operating of one's own free will.

My father said, "There even was a sign," surprising me still more. He usually decried such nonsense to me privately.

I said, "What sign was that then, Our Dad?"

Qualifying somewhat, he said, "At least it was a sign for me who finds that omens go by opposites. But I didn't mention it for obvious reasons to that superstitious crew up there."

"Mention what, Our Dad?"

"As how the day and date we met to make this Kingnap Plot was Friday the thirteenth."

CHAPTER 16
NOVEMBER 14 TO 17, 1936

Five days of feverish activity followed. On his rag-and-bone round, Barney broke hallowed precedent by calling, "Silks, satins and brocades," and astounded housewives with his generosity. He gave ten-pence-ha'penny for an old motheaten fur coat of Mrs. Hiatt's from the Old Cross Farm, tuppence here and thruppence there for lace and crochet work and bits of ripe and rotten velveteen. To pay for them, he drew out two pounds from his nest-egg in his Post Office Savings Bank account, a nest-egg earmarked for a visit home to Ireland in his golden years.

Practically every member of the Loyal Order made contributions to the decor of the urinal. All over Pontbran things turned up missing. Where had Aunty Rispa's feather boa gone? Old Lady Strong reported to the police she had been burgled of her new middle-kitchen net curtains. And my mother, going into her own bedroom, said, "This room looks different. Why?" The difference was, the printed imitation of a cross-stitch sampler above their bed, saying, "All Glory Laud and Honour to Thee Redeemer, King!" had disappeared. She never fathomed what she missed until she found it back in place the following week.

Perce Cook's wife caught him sneaking out with her best aspidistra, pot and all, and made him put it back, no questions asked. Risking being had on for unmentionable offences, grown men swiped bows and hair ribbons.

The quantities of women's frippery contributed suggested that the call was for something like the Rebecca Riots of a century before.

144

My father's interview with Clarence Makepiece took place in our potting shed.

"Jehovah, how Thy Name is Great," Clarence cried ecstatically. His lumpy yellow whites showed as he rolled his eyes. "I would gladly lay down my life to fight the good fight."

"No laying down your life involved," my father said. "That, in fact, is something to be avoided like the plague, if you want to do this cause some good. The most we want you risking is a year or so in stir."

"Ten, twenty years be not enough to give my God and King."

"Yes, well," my father said. "All we want for you to do is to stand up there and raise your voice to heaven. Just as you do on Saturday nights outside the pubs. Or riding on the Western Welsh to Newport. Your voice has got a lovely boom. It'd carry a long way. Would you like to do that for us, mate?"

"Amen! Hallelujah! Glory be to God Most High."

"You can say all that and more. The more the better."

"I have got that souvenir gun. I'll fire a couple of rounds into the air." The war apparently flashed back. His halo slipped. "Goddam Huns. Bloody Boche. I'll kill the bloody lot of them."

"You listen, now, Clarence. This is just to make a hullaballoo, no more. I don't want you running wild, doing things that you'll repent. On the other hand, you ent to do it if your heart ent in it. We don't want people saying that we took advantage of a simpleton. That we tricked or bullied you into doing it. It's got to be of your own free will. If you land up in the dock, you have to feel that it was worth the sacrifice."

For answer, Clarence snapped to attention and sang, "God Save the King" through twice before saluting. Then he grabbed the stove poker, slanted it across his shoulder and bawled, "Prese-ent Arms!" In another rapid shift, he went down on his knees, salaaming and intoning the Lord's Prayer.

My father said, "You can do it from the top of the Pantheon Cinema. We have arranged for the skylight to be left open down to the projection room. You can escape through that."

In those days the gunning down of leaders by revolutionaries and madmen wasn't as feared as it is now, so security was very lax. They didn't check out rooftops or keep tabs on wild, unstable types. So my growing apprehension was not on that account.

I said later to my father, "I hope, with all the strain, that that metal plate inside his head won't shift around and send Clarence off the deep end. I wouldn't like to see him doing something potty like jumping off the roof." (Or firing down into the crowds.)

"I have heard of funnier things happening, it is a fact," my father sighed. "But I have briefed him well. He has got it all down pat, including watching for the signal. We can only trust to God that it will all come off all right."

Adding greatly to their sense of drama and high mission was the reaction of South Wales' political leaders to the Tour. Among other Labour MPs, my father's hero, Aneurin Bevan, was reported in the *Argus* of November 17 as having sent the following letter to the Minister of Labour:

> "*Dear Mr. Brown:*
> *I learn from your letter that His Majesty intends to visit my constituency in the course of his visit to South Wales. You tell me that His Majesty proposes to visit the Social Centre in Rhymney and that I am invited to be present on that occasion. I should indeed like to show His Majesty the conditions under which our people are compelled to*

*live and to impress upon him the suffering inflicted on them
in consequence of the policy of his Ministers.*

*I cannot, however, associate myself with a visit which
would appear to support the notion that private charity
has or can ever make a contribution of any value to the
solution of the problems of the many measures which lie
within the power of the Government, and which I, in
common with my Parliamentary colleagues, have urged
from time to time.*

*Furthermore, His Majesty's visit takes place immediately
before the imposition of still further reduction in the
appallingly low allowances made to the unemployed of
South Wales.*

*I am sure it is not present in His Majesty's mind.
Nevertheless, it would seem that this visit may be used to
reassure the public mind that powerful sympathy is at last
being enlisted on behalf of our sorely oppressed people,
and that effective action is being taken to redress their
grievances. Yet how can this be so when even now the
administrative machinery is being prepared for the purpose
of adding to the burdens of those whose present plight
excites His Majesty's warm sympathy?*

*I deeply regret that His Majesty's well-known concern
for the unemployed should be used to mask not only the
negligence of his Ministers but their active persecution of
the poor. The Minister of Labour is the instrument of this
persecution.*

*The fact that this Minister proposes to accompany His
Majesty exposes the Crown to an odious association from
which wise statesmanship should protect it. In these circumstances, and for these reasons, I feel it is impossible
for me to be present to meet His Majesty on this occasion."*

Mr. Bevan's letter made you feel that members of Parliament

were real human beings. They tried harder, and aimed higher, for the common good. I took a fancy to his style: critical yet courteous, good for making a sly dig. I would try to copy it.

For this conversation, my father and I were in the garden hunting slugs and grubs. It was better not to hold discussion of this sort with my mother present. It only got her started on the necessity of my being more practical about my future. She had taken to nagging me lately about making friends with girls like Hester James's niece, Kathryn Swilling, who planned to follow in her auntie's footsteps as a teacher.

My father was of two minds about the letter. He was just as mad as Nye about the way the King was being used, but he didn't like the King being slighted. It was maiming the root to sucker the tree, in his opinion. "If you stay away to make a gesture or walk out in protest, you're not there to spread your influence in other ways," he explained to me.

Other political refinements could be picked up from the conduct of our own MP. It irked my father that he had failed to influence the King's itinerary. "It would have become him to have spoken out against them taking Him to the Grange." He meant: what had the Grange to do with the problems *we* were suffering? And why was our monarch to be driven along the pretty country road to Pontypool instead of up our grimy, shabby valley to see our poverty?

Like a limp handshake, it was in bad faith.

"If it wasn't for this little shindig we've cooked up," my father said, "the King would be no wiser leaving than he came."

The pressure was also mounting on the national scene. A crisis flared in Parliament over the lack of progress of the Special Areas Act. On Saturday, November 14, Commissioner Malcolm Stewart resigned, so-say on grounds of health. But his Third Report, published a few days earlier, betrayed his deep frustration. The Special Areas programme was a mockery. The Government had had those damning findings in their hands since summer, yet the new legislative programme contained no more than a perfunctory reference to the Act. Like all Mr. Stewart's previous suggestions, his last long list of recommendations had been flagrantly ignored.

On Tuesday, November 17, the Government faced revolt within its ranks. A group of Tory young turks joined with the Labour-Liberal opposition to bring pressure for a real improvement in the Act. But after an all-night tussle, this backbench uprising was quelled with false promises, and the do-nothing government once again prevailed.

Little did they know, but another opportunity would soon present itself, demanding such an extraordinary cross-party alliance. A constitutional crisis was even at that moment brewing. But in the end, the mavericks would once more fail to pool their power in support of the just cause.

The defusing of the Tory revolt had a profound effect on the conspiratorial brotherhood of the Loyal Order of the Prince of Wales. It gave an almost holy affirmation to their cause. It was as though they crouched once more in the last ditch on Gallipoli, holding the line in a life-and-death campaign.

Hindsight revealed later that a pyramid of ironies was building in those crucial days. All through the night of that furious debate in Parliament, the royal train was bearing the King to South Wales for his two-day tour. The King had previously invited Mr. Malcolm Stewart, as Commissioner for the area, to brief him on that journey. But, to the Government's great relief, Mr. Stewart bowed out before his pleas for support and action could gain dangerous access to the royal ear.

Instead, to the workers' loss (we found out when it was too late) the inexperienced new substitute Commissioner dined with the King on the royal train.

That was not the only cataclysmic issue boiling underneath the surface in those fateful days. Cover-ups were as rife as they are now. But the startling thing was that this cover-up was aided and abetted by the press itself. They conspired to gag themselves. Thanks to the power of discretion of the British newspaper barons and the BBC, which placed other considerations higher than the people's right to know, they totally blanked out certain crucial matters that concerned our King.

We would not learn until weeks later, after the die was cast, that even as He lay abed that clanking, rattling train, the King was bowed with awful problems of His own.

CHAPTER 17
NOVEMBER 18, 1936

Wednesday, November 18, while the Glamorgan people crowded into Pen-y-craig, Pontypridd, Merthyr Tydfil, Dowlais, Penrhiwceibr and Mountain Ash to catch a glimpse of their Most Gracious Sovereign whose token "touch" they hoped would cure them of their economic scrofula, all Monmouthshire prepared to crowd into Llantarnum, Pontbran, Pontypool, Blaenavon, Abertillery, and points between, the following day.

While the King trekked past mile upon desolate mile of Rhondda's grimy slag heaps and dingy strings of terrace houses, relieved only by arches of leeks from farms set up to occupy the unemployed, and by festoons of unlighted Davy lamps of long-idled miners, Gwent put up her flags and swept her streets in readiness, and everybody who was anybody took a bath.

And all the while the band of valiant conspirators worked around the clock to perfect their plan.

On the first morning of the tour (the Eve of our Great Day), my Uncle Jack, according to his version, "just happened into Cwmbran Gent's to take a leak," and found one there. "A bursted pipe was flooding out the place."

Like the good citizen he was, my Uncle Jack went straight across to Sergeant Rodney and reported it. Sadly harassed by the burdens that the King's impending visit imposed on him, the sergeant begged my uncle to do him a favour and fetch the plumber. Twm Sion Gruffydd, Sanitary Engineer, was fortunately in his shop. He answered duty's call at once.

He waded in the urinal with Sergeant Rodney to inspect the damage and turn off the cock. He stroked his chin as he examined the defective part. "I'm afraid that the particular fitting I do need for this connection, I will have to go to Newport for."

The Sergeant groaned. "Bad luck do always seem to run in batches. As if I haven't got enough to worry me."

"Never you mind," Twm Sion said sympathetically. "You just leave this to me, mun. I'll handle it. I'll just shut off the water and put this padlock on the door that I just happen to have with me, look. I'll keep the key myself and fix her up as soon as possible. No later than tomorrow, after all the rumpus of the King is over."

"Oh, *would* you, Mr. Griffiths? It is a nuisance it is out of use with all the crowds. But there it is. I am obliged to you."

"Think nothing of it. I'll just hang up these signs that I carry for emergencies like this. So nobody don't kick the door in inadvertent, say." The signs read: "Out of Order. Repairs in Progress", "Danger" and "Beware".

They expected that it would be pretty much plain sailing after that. My father, Ted Swilling, Bryn Thomas's Dad and others of the Kingnap band would come off work at two. All of them had swapped and juggled shifts to free themselves clear through into the following afternoon. A fair amount of money had undoubtedly changed hands.

All schools up the valley, barring Malpas who got only half a day, and Newport who were nowhere in it, were getting all of Thursday off. That didn't help me very much on Wednesday. The school train normally didn't get me home till four. And it crawled that afternoon, stopping to take on water, to observe adverse signals, even to pick up passengers at the Halt. The fact that the King's train would be coming down that line next day had probably upset routine.

When our train pulled into Pontbran Station, I was off
and running before it came to a full stop. I even had my
season ticket out to flash in case old red-tape Woods the
stationmaster happened to be at the gate. I didn't wait for
Bryn and Ruby, not just for eagerness to hotfoot it to the
scene of action. A more immediate, compelling reason was
that I'd been taken desperately short. Other people were
afflicted with the stomachache or nausea when they got
worked up. A touchy bladder was my own peculiar cross.

I knew I couldn't make it home without an accident. I
had to nip in somewhere fast. The Lanzos' was the most
convenient place, a bare rod, pole or perch beyond the
railway bridge. In the middle of the afternoon the place
was always on the quiet side. Nobody was in there scoffing
buns and tea.

When I pushed the door open, the bell brought Mrs. Lanzo
out from the back room. She was timid, aloof and seldom
seen. But Ben and his brother, who went to some R.C. school
down Newport way, were not yet home to mind the shop.

"Mrs. Lanzo, do you mind if I go out to your lav?" I was
shifting from foot to foot and scissoring my legs, so she
must have grasped my plight. Her enormous, sad, black eyes
regarded me intently, enigmatically, a moment. Finally she
nodded. I rushed along their passage and out the bailey
like a flash.

When I returned, Mrs. Lanzo was still standing where I'd
left her. She put me very much in mind of the Holy Mother
Mary with her bunned black shiny hair and smooth olive
skin. "Thank you. Thank you very much," I gushed. But she
just stood there, staring at me in a most peculiar way.

Mrs. Lanzo's English was extremely thin. But she did a
lot of speaking without benefit of tongue. She would flick
her chin and arch her Mediterranean brows to ask you what
you wanted and would hold up her fingers, one, two, three-
pence, if you asked the price.

Right then her eyes began to talk. Urgently and earnestly. She tossed her head towards her shoulder and looked back apprehensively.

"Someone's in the kitchen?" I translated, puzzled and a bit unnerved.

She shook her head and swanned her arm, up, over, further back.

"Something out the back you mean?"

Nod. Nod. "Si, Angelo."

I twitched my nose and frowned. "I didn't see him there."

She jerked her thumb indicating further back. "Chid. Chid."

I screwed my face up like a Pekinese. "Chid. Chid?" When I had repeated it a half a dozen times, it came to me. "Gosh, *shed*! Aye, aye."

Actually, the place she meant was a pretty substantial outbuilding where they made their frosty ice cream from a secret recipe they brought from Italy. It was also where they boarded Annabella and stored the hokey-pokey cart.

She nodded vigorously, her eyes round and compelling. Her intense gaze bade me to keep going. Her hands were fisted on the counter, her knuckles showing white.

"Angelo is out the shed," I said.

Nod, nod, nod-nod. Her fingers beckoned.

"He wants me to go down there?"

She reacted with alarm. Shake-shake, shake-shake her head went, ten a second.

I began to get the wind up. Things weren't quite right. "Do you want me to go out and fetch him for you, then?"

Shake-shake, shake-shake. "No, no."

She reached across the counter, caught hold of my arm and drew me close. She prodded my chest bone with her index finger, jerked her thumb across her shoulder, walked her finger-tips across the counter, cupped her hand around her ear, framed her mouth into a shush, and put her finger up and down across her lips. Her eyes begged me to understand. I saw distress and fear in them.

Was she asking me to go out there and eavesdrop on her nephew? Why?

Suddenly my throat went dry. I felt the blood drain from my face. Was Angelo with . . . Dear God, it couldn't be . . . She'd be at work this hour of the afternoon . . . It wasn't early closing day . . . But with our Muriel you never knew, silly gooby that she was.

I turned quickly to go out of the door.

Mrs. Lanzo waved me through, pressing her hands together palm to palm, praying secrecy and care.

When I peeped through the window of the Lanzos' shed, relief washed over me. Angelo was leaning with lithe nonchalance against the mangle-like contraption in which the Lanzos cranked their ice cream. His arm was casually draped around the top half of the wheel.

I was even more relieved to see Emrys Strong squatting on the hokey-pokey's shafts.

And curiouser and curiouser, sitting on an up-turned crate was a small dark stranger with anthracite-bright eyes. He looked like one of the the half-starved little chaps I had seen once down the Pill, hanging around the Seaman's Mission and the fly-blown cafés, next door to reeking doorways of boarded-up shops. In our idle ports, the foreign-born couldn't get work and couldn't get home because they couldn't get work, was the way my father put it. First refusal even of the meanest jobs on board and on the docks had to go to British workers, if the owners were to get their government handouts. You may have lived there all your life, but if you weren't a citizen you didn't stand a chance.

It was clear there was no amorous assignation involving my dumb sister. So why would Mrs. Lanzo send me out to spy? At first blush it seemed a dirty trick to play on her own flesh and blood. I carried on listening.

My ear began to get accustomed to the muffled conversation going on behind the glass and brick. The first word I caught was "pill". Then "boat . . . row . . . dark." With a shock I caught on that they were talking about some kind of jiggery-pokery involving boats.

Many were the tales my father told me of the smuggling of contraband along our coastline of the Severn Estuary and Bristol Channel. How, in days of yore, on still, moonless nights, muffled oars would carry to shore unexcised cargos of wine, spirits and tobacco from the Continent. If they had done it then, I reckoned they could do it now. Where Angelo was concerned, anything was possible.

From my cock-eyed, wry-necked stance, I could make out money passing hands, coins and a pound note. "T'en much," said Emrys. "Wish to hell that we could manage more."

"I'm not doing it for money," said the sailor in his soft-pedal voice. "It is the principle. The bloody English. Even the score."

Angelo shifted from his perch. "Well, that's about it. You sure you got it straight?"

"The boat's already spoken for," the sailor said. "I pay him this and it is set."

Angelo smiled and moved towards him with snaky grace. He put his arm about the bony shoulders, giving them a comrade's squeeze. "You'll do, my friend. Your day of reckoning is not far off."

The sailor appeared to be moved. He gave his hand to shake his bond and said goodbye.

I was in a vulnerable position. The best cover I could find was a rain barrel.

Emrys came out with the sailor. "There'll be a train down shortly, mate." They struck out for the station.

I didn't dare emerge while Angelo was there. My nerves jangled, my body shivered with cold and apprehension, as I waited. At last, standing it no longer, I craned around the barrel to spy out the land. I was about to creep along the bailey, when, suddenly, looking foxier than usual, Tich appeared. He went inside the outbuilding.

My curiosity did battle with my fears, and won. Like a shot, I was back, peering through the smeared, cobwebby glass. Tich's arm was stuck out Mussolini-style. He even pugged his face and doubled his chin, *Il-Duce* fashion. "All set?" he said.

Angelo put out his cigarette. "Uh-Huh. That ugly little chap will row the boat up Black Monk Pill around high tide tonight. He and Emrys think it is to row over to the Gloucester side to throw the coppers off the scent. Emrys is a gullible old ass. He isn't hard to fool."

"And the rest of the arrangements, sir?" Sir, was it now!

"The trawler will be standing offshore waiting for our signal. When they respond, we'll row right out."

"Where will they take him, sir?"

"That isn't your affair. Yours is not to question why."

"I hope they don't rough-handle him, is all. After all, he is our King."

Long before then I should have twigged who the "him" they were referring to must be. But when Tich said "King" I nearly died of shock.

In a flash, I saw I had stumbled on a counterplot. Not just a counterplot, mind you, but a combination counterplot and double-cross. Conspiracy within conspiracy. Like those carved ivory trinkets from the East, a box within a box within a box.

Fate, aided and abetted by us trusting fatheads, had put Angelo literally in the driver's seat to work a counter-snatch. What bill of goods had Emrys Strong been sold to join with him? That they would only hold the King here on English soil, and only until some of their political demands were satisfied?

And all the while the fascist lot planned a double-twist. What did they have in store for Edward VIII? What would happen to the British nation with him gone? I recalled my father's comment on how wise Lord Kitchener had been refusing to allow the King (then Prince of Wales) to fight in the Great War – not simply for the Prince's personal good but to protect the country's high morale. The same thing now. To put our country in a turmoil or a constitutional crisis was something Nazi Germany and Fascist Italy would love to do. With us distracted, their attacks on helpless nations would go unchallenged, as would their wholesale programme of rearmament.

In the same instant, I realised that Angelo most likely had yet another double-cross worked out. He would doubtless ditch Tich Veasy as soon as Tich had served his purpose. And what was to become of Emrys and the poor deluded sailor? Worse yet, what would happen to Obie with the King inside the van? My scalp began to crawl as if it were alive with lice. I saw then why the loyal, honourable Mrs. Lanzo had felt driven to tell on her own kin.

Angelo was saying, "Now just remember, soldier, if anything goes wrong with our end, the Blaenavon Cenotaph alternative goes into play. If I am incapacitated, it will be up to you to get the word through that Plan B is on. You will not fail. Your oath is sealed in blood."

It would have sounded like pure melodrama if it weren't for the fanatic gleam in Tich's eyes. And the queasy feeling in my gut.

As soon as it seemed safe, I scuttled off as fast as quaking legs would carry me.

There was nobody at home. My mother had left a note propped on the mantelpiece between the caddy and the clock: "Your dinner is in the oven, put the guard back round the fire, the last two hundredweight have sparked. Do not let the dog in. I have scrubbed and polished for tomorrow. Come straight on down your Auntie Phyllis's. I'm helping decorate her house."

I gulped a couple of hunks of meat and parsnip, more to keep me going than out of any appetite. I caught the first bus I could manage, but not to Auntie Phyllis's.

My first call was the bakery. When I asked him where my father was, Mr. Vowles slapped flour off his hands and whispered, "I don't expect him until later when they come to do the van."

I looked up Leonard Hasty at the station. He told me *sotto voce* through the ticket grille, "They're meeting shortly in the Old Crown pub."

There was half an hour to go till opening time.

It was a dark and chilly evening. The air smelt damp and seaweedy as though a storm was blowing in. If we had rain, all the red, white, and blue paper bunting would collapse in a bedraggled soggy purple pulp.

To keep out of the wind I hung around the entrance to the Pantheon Cinema with its big billboards about Laurel and Hardy and the even more ridiculous Three Stooges. I crouched against a poster announcing that the mannish-voiced, boy-chested Greta Garbo would be "Coming Shortly". I was shivering with cold and trepidation.

At last I saw my father going up the ramp into the Old Crown pub.

I called to him.

"Name of God," he said. "You are supposed to go down to your Auntie Phyllis's."

"I got to talk to you, our Dad."

"Not now, lass. I am rushed clear off my feet." He sheepishly jerked his head towards the pub. "We ent going in to booze, you know. We had to have a place to meet."

"I have got to tell you something, our Dad."

"Then speak up, Viddy, girl. I'm not stopping you."

"Not here, though. Somewhere private."

My manner finally got through to him that the news I had to tell was serious. "Jerusalem," he said, alarmed. "Now what have you gone and done?"

"I haven't done nothing –"

"Our Mu, is she all right?"

I whispered, "It's about the Kingnap Plot."

"Hisht! Shut your bleeding trap."

He darted a swift look around and briskly headed me toward the canal bridge and down onto the bank. The mist swirled around us like a smoke-filled tavern. The cold seeped through my threadbare, outgrown overcoat. I delved my hands deep into the patched and cobbled pockets.

"Now," my father said. "And kindly keep your voice down. You don't know who is up ahead all ears."

I told him everything. He didn't interrupt. But I sensed him stiffen as I hit the double, then the double-double cross. He asked me several questions at the end.

We had walked as far as Two Locks Bridge and back again by time I finished. He leaned against the clammy stones under the Pontbran arch and mopped his face. I waited, freezing. At last he said, "I think you had better come with me to tell the others, Vid."

Me being a minor and a girl, they wouldn't let me in the Old Crown pub. My father fetched Nwd and Obie out. He explained to them, "Our Viddy just told me something that we all should hear. Twm and Ted are in the Gents preparing. We shall go in there."

Nwd flashed a message with his eyes that I was not

supposed to see. He muttered something, probably concerning the propriety of my entering a lavatory reserved for Gentlemen.

My father said testily, "Don't make difficulties, Nwd. What odds is it? We have got enough to do with as it is."

Catching on from this that something serious was afoot, Nwd looked alarmed. "All right," he said. "I'll go ahead and warn them. Take care. Come one by one. Remember we are right under them blasted bobbies' noses." Light streamed out of the doorway of the red brick police station and barely missed the Gents.

In the dim light of a couple of candles, I took in everything at once. But my nose took precedence over my eyes. For all poor Twm Sion Gruffydd had worked his fingers to the bone all afternoon, the smell inside the urinal shouted louder than a megaphone.

I suppose no amount of scrub and scour, soap and water, disinfectant and pure elbow grease could have washed away the odours of a couple of generations of hard-drinking men. The stench was trapped inside a million tiny pits and pores eaten into the metal. The cast iron stalls were permeated through and through.

I said, "Pooh!" involuntarily and wrinkled up my nose.

Poor Twm Sion's face, which had been wreathed in self-congratulatory smiles, collapsed. "What is it?"

"Still pongs a bit." I had the chivalry to understate the case and look apologetic for my breach.

"No!" said Twm in that blaming, disbelieving tone my mother often used, to try to talk me out of facts she hoped would go away if she disavowed them. "No! Never in the world! It do smell as sweet as a baba's breath, I swear."

"More like a baba with a nappy-full," said Ted Swilling, his clean-up assistant, not meaning to be cruel, just to show his wit.

My father quickly intervened, "But there is lovely that it looks. You have done marvels."

I had never been inside a Gents before. Such an extraordinary privilege. Its geography was different from the usual water closet, albeit substantially disguised right now. The decoration was quite far along. A tiger rug hung over one partition, the body somewhat mangy, but the magnificent head still beautifully preserved. Mrs. Hiatt's moleskin coat was draped across another. There were several elaborate displays of fruit and flowers, placed to match off the corners, and interesting stuffed bird and beast arrangements.

Gorgeous lace drapery and shiny stuffs covered the broad expanse of ugly metal walls. Immediately ahead of the front door was a banner that Twm Sion had borrowed from the Band of Hope. Silver letters on a blue ground read ambiguously: "Fear Not the Lord is with You." It was meant to reassure His Majesty.

In the middle urinary was a basket chair covered with a red plush tablecloth. The throne. Above it hung my mother's sampler, proclaiming "All Glory, Laud, and Honour To Thee Redeemer King." Considering the handicaps it was all quite elegant, if a little on the gaudy side. Everything deserved a tick – except the overpowering smell of addled eggs, strong fish and gorgonzola cheese combined.

Obie made a noble effort when he entered, fiercely refusing to let any olfactory reaction show on his face. Had he remarked, "A bit heavy in here, isn't it?" or given a little whistled "phew", I would have felt a good deal easier. His very reticence confirmed how bad it really smelt.

"He won't be in here but a couple of seconds," my father said to resolve it quickly. "We can sprinkle some scent around. My Missus keeps some on the dressing table. Essence of lilacs, p'raps lily of the valley."

"Eau de cologne, mind, would be posher. More cut glass," said Nwd. "Or even camphorated oil. I also like a spot of eucalyptus on my handkerchief, especially when my head's bunged up."

Crushed, Twm Sion said, "My sense of sniff must all be gone. I cannot smell it for the life of me."

"Working in it all the time, you don't," Ted said. "The nose gets used to it."

My father said, "Well, as it happens, that is the smallest of our worries. The girl here brings some serious news. It could put a big crimp in our tail."

Ted speculated, scared, "Have them bleeders over the road got wind of us?" He thumbed in the direction of the police station.

"Worse than that," my father said. "There is treason and sedition in our ranks."

In whispers, I retold my story. Twm Sion appeared to take it worst. He even swore. "*Yr hen diawl*. The old foreign divil."

"Emrys and Tich ent foreigners," reminded Nwd, "and they're as bad."

Said Twm, "That *mwchen*, Angelo, have played on Emrys's cantankerousness and Tich's folly." He let rip in a stream of Welsh. His eyebrows looked like bushes on an overhanging cliff.

Nwd said, "Is Angelo really serious?"

"For sure," Obie said. "This is no game. Remember that story in the *Herald*: That Italian warship? Their crew lining up to pee down on a British lighter? They're just looking for an opening."

My usefulness exhausted after detailed cross-examination, they tried to slough me off like an old shoe. "Your mother will be worrying," my father canted. "You run along now like a good girl." When I objected, he got cross. "It is no good showing off. I am in no mood for any lip. There's a big decision facing me."

I stayed awake till far into the night. My brain felt like rough ground, newly ploughed and harrowed. I realised the consequences of our decisions were enormous. Even though others had twisted our plan, subverting our intentions, we were still responsible for its unfolding. It was still our creature. We still had to come up with a resolution.

I wished we had never got into such a stupid situation. I wished my father had never had so daft a mumpy. How much easier to do nothing, to sit back and shovel blame elsewhere. Let others sort it out.

But my twig was already bent. I was my father's daughter. I had turned too far towards his light. I was stuck with his stubborn will to action and the obligations that went along with it.

I tossed and flapped, waiting for him to come home with answers. Every so often I fancied I could hear the front door opening. It could only have been night creaks, however, or the moaning of the wind. Once I could have sworn he stumbled on the worn patch in the stair carpet. But it was only our Muriel chortling in her dreams.

My bed got hard and lumpy and my mind grew feverish from fighting sleep. It began to seem as if the Kingnap plot itself, to say nothing of the revelations of the double switches, were nightmare fantasies. Round and round spun images of knaves and kings and joker-executioners, down and down into a sucking vortex, receding and diminishing to hop-o'-my-thumbs – which suddenly and monstrously dilated into bloated giants, snapping me awake with fear. And I would know again that it was all too true, and a trap door in my stomach would unlatch and drop my innards through.

What would the Loyal Brotherhood decide? Would they work still another switch of endings? How? Would they lock the three counter-plotters up until it was all over? If so, who would drive the van? And how could they avert the Blaenavon Cenotaph alternative?

I had no idea what to pray for, for the best.

CHAPTER 18
NOVEMBER 19, 1936

The next thing I remember, my sister Muriel was shaking me awake. "Get up, lazybones. If you turn over and go back to sleep, it's your lookout. I'm not calling you again." In a half-dozed way, I thought I had got rid of her. But suddenly she yelled, "Now, come on. Out of it!" She stripped the bedclothes off my back in one violent swoop.

Swearing my whole repertory of curses, I lashed out angrily, but she dodged my scramming hands and fled. Outside the door, she delivered her parting shot, "It'll be your own fault if you miss the King!"

Then it all came back to me and I shot up like a jumping jack.

It was not a very special day. Dull, cold and greyish as though a soft-coal fire gave off a thick pale smoke that settled ash-flakes over everything. About the only good thing you could say was that the rain held off.

"I don't know where your father's got to," my mother said, dishing up the porridge. "He never did come home last night, the fool. I shall have a nice big bone to pick with him. What, in the name of all that's holy, they are making all that fuss for, I can't conceive. The King will have come and gone in half a minute."

"Ditto," I said softly. I meant, why had she spent the best part of yesterday helping decorate the front of Auntie Phyllis's? The King wouldn't pass that way.

The village heaved with people when we got there. Thursday,

November 19, 1936, was the occasion for the only brush with history that the vast proportion of the area's residents felt they would ever have. There was an unstated feeling in the air that being part of the great crowd scene in that spectacle would save them from oblivion.

It was touch and go whether we would have found a decent place from which to see His Majesty if some fat old lady's ill wind hadn't blown us three a bit of good. Just as we passed, gloomily concluding we would have to settle for a craning view from the back side of the crowd, she up and swooned from having stood there half the night. The space vacated when they hauled her off was just right for the three of us. "Front row, upper circle," bragged my mother. Indeed it was. We faced the cinema. The public lavatory lay slightly to our left and in good view.

Elementary school children all wearing tams lined the roads. They carried threepenny Woolworths' paper Union Jacks. Made by the Japs. A lot of them also had home-crayoned Welsh flags, their red dragons variously resembling hippopotamuses and giraffes. Self-important teachers paraded up and down in front of them, making sure of grandstand views.

In two long lines down the middle of the street stood the Honour Guard. In freshly whitinged belts and straps, the St. John's Ambulance contingent looked uniformly smart, as usual. Also in spruce form were the Salvation Army and the Fire Brigade. The remainder was a mufti'd mixture of bemedalled ex-servicemen representing the British Legion and old soldiers. Stationed in a body near the urinal, their three-feathered emblems sticking proudly from their button-holes, was the entire membership – certain principals excepted – of the Loyal Royal Order of the Prince of Wales.

"Where is our Dad, then, our Mam?" my sister said.

"Don't ask *me*, love. Who am I to know?"

I glanced towards the urinal. The door was closed. Was he waiting in the wings for his cue to play the role of his career?

My mother said, "And where is Obadiah Dixon? I would have thought, them two being ringleaders, they'd be right in front."

Before I had recovered from her alarming choice of epithet, she said, "Good Gracious me! Nor Clarence Makepiece isn't there. I never would have thought *he'd* miss a chance like this."

I sneaked a casual glance up to the opposite roof. Was he lurking down behind the mock front gable? Or had they called the whole thing off?

She continued fretting about where my father was, so to lull her curiosity, I said, "Maybe he is at the station going to be introduced."

"With knobs on. Although I don't know why he wouldn't have just as much right to the honour as Colonel this and Captain that, who are total strangers to this area."

Our Muriel craned above the crowd. Following her gaze, I sighted part of Vowles's van. It was backed up to the far side of the Gents, the bonnet headed in the planned direction. Like the coalhouse door on stormy nights, my heart began to bang. The Kingnap Plot must still be on.

A second later, I saw what had attracted her attention: Angelo. He appeared to be wiping the van's windscreen clear of morning fog. My heart slammed violently. Those stupid trusting idiots! Had they told him they were on to him and given him a second chance?

"What is the matter with you, Viddy? You are like a wireworm with nerves. For goodness sake stand still."

I had just caught sight of Tich standing on the running board. Where was Emrys? Blessed Lord.

That was all the time I had for speculation. Lookouts

passed the word that the royal train was coming round the bend. The shoulders of the Loyal Order tightened visibly. Uncle Jack clutched the Loyal Order's standard, the giant Welsh Dragon, as though his life depended on it – as well it might.

A momentary hush fell on the crowd. We could hear the train as it pulled into the station. It hissed to a dead stop. Distant cheers rang out, and singing, too. Anticipation rustled through the crowd, swelling to a rhubarb of excitement. Necks craned, eyes popped. Excruciating minutes passed.

At last, around the corner of the rise, the glinting muzzle of a motor car appeared. It crawled between the first ranks of the bristling Honour Guard.

All hell broke loose.

The King had come.

The King had come.

Flimsy flags waved frantically. Little lungs hip-hip-hoorayed to bursting point. Even grown-ups shouted themselves hoarse. Chapel deacons pranced and jumped. Teachers leaned and shoved their elbows in their charges' eyes. Ogling parents accidentally knocked their kiddies' tams over their faces at the crucial instant that the King went by. The mass-bands boomed and sawed "*Mae Hen Wlad Fy Nhadau*" then "God Save the King", putting heart and soul in it.

The car was nearly on us. There were too many things to keep an eye on. I could barely spare a glance for Edward VIII to see him in real flesh and blood. My attention was now riveted on Uncle Jack.

Just as the royal car nosed into the dense avenue of Loyal Order men, the standard dipped as though in homage. This was the signal for Clarence's red-herring ploy. The Honour Guard closed ranks, screening off the royal car. A seething mass surged into the clear space behind them, cutting off our view. Behind us people shoved and pushed, carrying us along.

At the same moment, reports like exploding crackers resounded from the roof of the Pantheon Cinema. Clarence Makepiece hove into view. He windmilled strenuously, then blew his trumpet fit to fell the Walls of Jericho. As at a tennis match, a sea of heads turned in an instant all in the same direction. The plot was on.

The surging, deafening mob prevented me from seeing or hearing what was happening at the hub of action. I guessed the muster of conspirators was tightly huddled around the car. My heart thumped harder than the pumps at Sudbrook bailing out the seepage from the Severn Tunnel. I saw the car roof moving slowly on . . .

The crowd went wild with jubilation. It heaved and wriggled like a sack of maggots in the socket of a dead sheep's eye.

I struggled to stay upright.

The car crawled out of sight beyond the urinal.

The hubbub and the melee was augmented by the hullaballoo inside my head. I had lost my mother and sister in the crush, and was wedged between an Amazon and a navvy with a tot seated on his shoulder. The tot squirmed, poking her flagstick in his Adam's apple. She nearly got my eye with the other end. "Where's the King to, our Dad?" she whined.

Her father said, "Why, lovely bud! That was the King that just went by. The man that waved."

"What man? I didn't see nobody in a golden crown."

"No love. He didn't have one. He is just like any other man."

Her face collapsed. "I want to see the King."

"Too late, now, love. He have gone on down in that big motor car."

Had he? I thought. Or was he even now penned up inside the Gents, with Obie talking earnestly to put his mind at rest?

And was that King of England now on display in the big swanky Daimler no other than my father, Fred E. Williams?

That was when I saw the flash of Vowles's van pulling out beyond the mob. It could only mean that the transfer of His Majesty out of the Gents' had been completed. My heart missed beats like the notes that wouldn't play on my Auntie Blod's melodeon. It was all the proof I needed that the snatch, as planned, was under way.

My reaction was pure dread. Why would they have ignored my warning of Angelo's machinations? What would happen to the King now? More to the point, what would become of my poor Dad?

The kid who missed the King began to sob her heart out. I couldn't help thinking we'd all be better off if my father and the Loyal Order had missed him too. Sad, perhaps, but safe.

But I had no time to dwell on forlorn wishes or regrets. I had two immediate, urgent actions on my mind. First I had to get across that milling crowd to the ladies outhouse of the Old Crown pub.

As luck would have it, the whole heaving mass suddenly broke into song: a great spontaneous surge of glorious sound. "Among our ancient mountains/God Bless the Prince of Wales" and then "Guide me O Thou Great Jehovah", all parts in harmony. There is no better form of crowd control. Everyone stood still.

I managed to wend my way across. And none too soon. I had to break the queue outside the WC, and suffer the consequence of evil looks, though I'd asked them nicely if they wouldn't mind.

Coming out, I passed the cinema. I was relieved to see old P.C. Wiley reading Clarence Makepiece the riot act. The signs were good that he was getting off with just a dressing down.

My second urgent mission was to find my Uncle Jack. Unfortunately my mother found him first. She was asking him where my father was.

"He went to Pontypool," said Uncle Jack. "There is a rally of old comrades of the Welsh Guards and the Royal Welsh Fusiliers to meet the King. It is in the yard of Park Gate Garage about half-past ten. Fred thought we ought to have a representative detachment of the Loyal Order there. Him and Obie and a couple more have gone for that." A grand job of covering he did.

"He might just let me know when he takes it in his head to do such things."

My eyes bored into Uncle Jack like wimbles. "Did it all go off as planned?" I asked him cryptically.

"Aye, aye. It did. Right down to the last detail. Now all we got to do is wait until your Dad comes back to hear about the other part." He winked with lightning rapidity offside from my mother. "Don't worry. It'll work out beautiful."

But I did worry. Terribly. Try as I would to pump the Brethren, I couldn't get a line on what was going on. In the first place, those I contacted were as close as clams. They must have had branded on their brains what they'd be in for if a word leaked out.

But perhaps it wasn't just caution that locked their tongues. I got the distinct impression that those I talked to, like Bryn Thomas's father, knew nothing about the counterplot. They all seemed to be exuding satisfaction that everything had gone according to the *original* plans.

I simply couldn't get the inside of my head together. I was unsettled, fidgety, like birds before a storm. My mother wanted me to accompany her and our Muriel to Auntie Phyllis's. But I claimed that Uncle Jack had asked me to go up on my season ticket to take the standard to the rally at the Park Gate Garage in Pontypool. It was true that the top of the valley was my intended destination. But my real secret reason for going there was to find out as soon as possible if His Majesty was safe and back on schedule for the Pontypool/Blaenavon leg of his itinerary. If I could determine that, my uneasiness would largely disappear.

More than that, I had had a sudden wave of dread that I hadn't sufficiently emphasized the threat of Angelo's Plan B: the Blaenavon Cenotaph Alternative. Even if they had blocked Angelo's ploy, would they have enough sense to stop Tich signaling the hitch in plans to his Blackshirt cronies up the valley? I owed it to my father, King and country to go and be on the *qui-vive* at the Blaenavon ceremonies.

More easily thought than done, however. There is no point here recounting the frustrations of that journey. Enough to say that by time the interrupted railway schedule permitted me to put in an appearance, the royal wreath already decked the cenotaph. To my very great relief, I learned that the Royal Self was miraculously unscathed. It was a double gladness, too, to know that whatever action the Loyal Brotherhood had achieved that day, it had affected neither His Majesty's security nor his aplomb. What if – oh, what if – I hardly dared to hope for it – the snatch had worked, and they had gained the Royal Ear and won his confidence for a few vital minutes?

What happened next convinced me that this indeed had been the case. When I caught up with the royal entourage, I was in time to hear His Majesty speak His famous words justifying all our faith in Him. Instead of a wasted journey, I was favoured to be a witness to His historic speech.

I know the newspapers reported that the celebrated exclamation occurred elsewhere, in another dismal context of ruin and decay. But that's newspapers for you; always getting things mixed up and turned around. I know they got *this* wrong. Or else He said the same thing in two places.

I even have a picture from the paper of Him talking to the shabby unemployed old sods He said it to. The proof that I was there is the blurred blob in the top right corner background of the picture. If you look hard you can make out a foot dangling from a lamppost. The boot and sock are mine. It was on that perch, a couple of seconds before some bobby yanked me down, that I had the privilege of looking the King directly in the eye as He gathered His shocked thoughts.

Those eight words are burnt into my memory. They said reams more than any of the fancy formal speeches others put into His mouth. He said, "Something must be done. Something *will* be done."

Something must be done. Something *will* be done. Well, there it is.

CHAPTER 19
NOVEMBER 20 TO DECEMBER 2, 1936

I hurried home to share my pleasure with my father. I could hardly wait to hear whether his mumpy had at last been satisfied, and borne the sweet fruit of the King's pronouncement. But he hadn't yet returned, and I began having real misgivings about how he'd fared.

I tried to hold the lid on my imagination by keeping busy. My father had piled up a backlog of routine chores during his preoccupation with the Kingnap plot. Night frosts were threatening, so I chopped some stick and riddled ashes saved from the kitchen fire to salvage coke for the greenhouse stove.

When my chest began to feel it had a band around it, I tried locating other members of the Loyal Order, to try to pry the truth from them. But those I collared were clearly as ignorant as I was. Curious, but not the least bit worried, just peckish for some news. They figured those not present and accounted for were off celebrating somewhere. They seemed to think this absence a good sign.

But I didn't. I was now scared to death that the whole thing had misfired. What if my father had been caught red-handed in the very act of Kingnapping? I was terrified he was being held behind bars somewhere incommunicado and me not raising a finger to free him.

When the not-knowing got unbearable, it came to me that I hadn't asked Ted Swilling. He had been present in the Gents during my reporting of Angelo's betrayal. I tracked him down out on the back lane.

He told me that after my departure, they had stood helpless for a while, trying to process my bad news.

As the implications of the treachery sank in, my father had found himself vexed beyond enduring. That "sodding swine" Angelo and "them two stupid buggers" who had swallowed his hook, had thrown a spanner in the works of his most cherished hopes.

He sat down on the throne, scrubbing his scalp with callused fingers, while all present in the Gents vented and chewed the matter over in graveyard tones.

The obvious defeatist view came first, put forward by Ted Swilling. "It's all over, en it? Have to call off the whole bloody thing."

Twm Sion let out a growl of pain. He had too much of himself invested in it to let it go. "Got to catch the divils and put them under lock and key until we're done."

My father said, "But how do we know that more of them blackshirt blighters ben't out there, waiting to take over? Like our Viddy said, the bastards talked about a Blaenavon alternative. God knows what they'd do to Him up there."

"Better for us to keep hold of the reins," said Nwd.

Obie, who had been quiet, cogitating, up till then, said gravely, "I say again, this is not any little game or stunt. We have put our sovereign in mortal danger. These men are a real threat, and we have handed them their opportunity. We must forget our own ambitions and concentrate on the safety of the King."

Everyone was quiet. My father put his hands over his face to hide the surge of disappointment welling up in him. He had placed so much importance on this moment, the culmination of his life-long mumpy, it would be wrenching to forego it. Of course, he knew his duty. If he had to relinquish his own hopes to protect the King, that's what he would do. "Fair enough, Obe. If our aims are putting Him at risk, it is up to us to keep Him out of it." But inwardly he couldn't help hoping against hope that some way could be found to modify their plot, to keep him safe *and* talk to him.

Obie said, "The thing to do is trick them like they think they're tricking us – with a counter-counterplot." When nobody said anything he went on, "Just as they are countermining our plot, we shall countermine *their* counterplot with another double twist."

"Oh, there is brilliant, Obe," my father breathed. Though circumstances might alter goals, there would be some satisfaction in outsmarting those who did them dirt.

The Executive Committee retreated to the back room of the Old Crown to spin and weave the counterplot. Only a few hours remained to slip over to the Vowles's parlour for a brief doss down before it was time to launch the action. Here Ted supplemented with hearsay from Nick Vowles.

A full shift of work, the many hours of preparation, and the energy required to come up with a counter-counterplot left my father bleary-eyed and wobbly as he began his toilet in the predawn hour. Only nervous excitement and dedicated purpose carried him along.

In the Vowles's back kitchen he had a good wash, as a king might do. For his latest haircut he had told the barber to give him a royal trim and it only needed wetting down. Despite his trembling fingers he gave himself a close shave without a nick. In a starched shirt, his best suit and a dark overcoat, topped by a bowler, he thought he was a good match to the recent pictures of the King he had cut out of the *Daily Mail*. He was satisfied he could deceive the sharpest eye.

Did that mean, I asked Ted, that the main part of the original plot continued to go forward? But he didn't know, and I returned home as frustrated as I left.

I shall never forget those hours of sweating. I sank very

low in spirits. I kept thinking of all the disobedient things I'd done to irk him. I vowed never to give him one further minute of vexation if only he came back to us. I think that was my first experience of what might remotely bear the name of genuine prayer.

As the day wore on, I found it harder by the minute to bridle my anxiety. When my mother came home, it was harder still. I had to keep reassuring her that his absence wasn't sinister. No doubt, I said, he had dropped in for a couple on "Pub Row" in Pontypool to celebrate. I waggishly forecast that he'd come staggering home around midnight.

He did come staggering home some time after darkness fell. But not the worse for drink. A group of butties bore him like a warrior, wounded but triumphant, from the battlefield.

In mind, if not in action, I fell upon my knees and thanked the Lord heartfeltly for his safe return, despite the fact his noble nose was battered to a bloody pulp, to ruin for ever his resemblance to his paragon.

The story, for my mother, was that he got bested in a tipsy brawl. It was obvious I'd have to wait until a good night's sleep had restored his vigour, and cold compresses reduced his swollen face, before I got the proper story. Just from his condition, I knew things hadn't exactly gone to plan. But the silence of the wireless and press suggested he had not, at least, come into dangerous conflict with authority, and that was all I cared about right then. It was enough to have him home.

Next morning, after his tea, he seemed in better shape and spirits. I followed him down the greenhouse and joined him nipping buds and side shoots off his prize chrysanthemums to make them saucersize for Christmas. Still saying nothing, he raised the cover of the stove and peered inside. "You are a good girl lighting it against the frost last night," he said, adding flashing stick and coke. "We could have lost a lot of plants. I couldn't have a better right hand if you'd've been a son." It was the highest compliment he could bestow on me, if a bit double-edged.

Screwing up my face I whined, "Aw, come on, Our Dad, my tongue is hanging out."

He laughed. "It isn't good enough to keep you in suspense, is it?" he said, relenting. "Especially as you were the one to save the day." Well, where'll us start?" And he began unravelling all that took place after they had dispatched me from the Gents.

He was snuffling like Uncle Jack, and had great difficulty speaking. But I got the gist. And so began a saga that would grow over many lifetimes, told in many versions, authorised and apocryphal.

Before the false dawn, he and Obie snook over to the Gents for the long wait. They eased the stress by rehearsing the upcoming strategy over and over to get it perfect. They listened with every ounce of concentration for cues from the sounds outside.

The noises of the assembling crowd grew to a loud hum that filled the air. Against this background, they had to strain to hear the line-up of the Loyal Order's Honour Guard. On the basis of a need-to-know, only those closest to the urinal had been filled in on the change in plans.

They listened with pricked ears for Vowles's van to pull up outside the exit. At the pulsing racket of the engine, the slam of doors and Angelo's voice, they exchanged affirming glances. The stage was set, the huge cast ready and assembled, the lead waiting in the wings and my father with as bad a case of stage fright as any leading man who ever lived.

At last they heard the train puffing down the line into the station. The next few minutes seemed like an age. The crescendo of the crowds' roar informed them that the royal car had come in sight and was moving slowly down the road.

Their cue, the command to present arms, rang in their ears. They listened for Clarence's distracting rumpus – sharp cracks and a bugle call. They heard the crowd's collective "Aw" in surprised response. *This was it.*

Obie nodded. My father steeled himself. In another instant he dived out of the urinal into the scrum of the Loyal Order's Honour Guard. He plunged into the milling tangle where P.C. Conkle had suddenly lost control.

The pinnacle of my father's lifelong mumpy had arrived. But it came and went in a split second. He had only the most fleeting, bitter-sweet glance inside the car. The figure in the back sat like a photograph, flat and still. The car doors remained closed. The Daimler went inching forward.

Under cover of the commotion, my father ducked back through the squirming crowd the way he came. He popped straight back into the urinal and History slipped down the other side.

At this point in my father's tale, I should have been feeling elation. This was the moment when the prince met the pauper. If this had been fiction, there would be a crossing, to give a satisfying climax to the story. But history doesn't work that way. It rambles on, falls flat and fizzles. Nothing happened between my father and the King.

My emotions plunged – the let down, the disappointment, was overwhelming. What upset me most was the unfairness. After so many failed attempts my father deserved success. But here, once more, his dream was failing him. I had to purse my lips to stop them trembling. I was afraid I'd break down if I glanced at him.

But my father went on without pause. Angelo and company had no inkling of the sleight of hand. With the vital exception that the switch had been aborted, the detailed moves of the original plan remained intact.

My father, in his role as Kingnapped King, was steered by Obie into the waiting van. Tich assisted, bowing and scraping as he closed the door.

As the van drove off, they sat face to face as though engrossed in the planned chinwag. They kept this up as they drove along in case Angelo happened to look back.

My father and Obie had every reason to exchange earnest glances. Everything had gone according to their secret counter-counter-plan. They saw their failure as success. If their hopes to reach the King's ear had been scrubbed, the nobler goal to save Him and the country had been won.

So far, so good. Now they had to get away. They had figured out another ending to the modified scenario. Obie had reasoned they could wait until the van slowed down in traffic. Then they would open the door, jump out and make a run for it.

When they came to Whitehorse Pitch, they felt the van decelerate and shift down to take the gradient. They lunged towards the door. But it wouldn't yield. Tich had locked them in.

Dismayed my father said, "What now, Obie?"

"If we hammer on the panel, and let them grasp it's only you and me, they'll see their plan is ruined. I doubt they can do much to us in a built-up area like this."

But no amount of banging brought them to a halt. Angelo must have assumed that the King himself, with Obie, would kick up ructions on discovering the trap. The van drove on to a lonely place near Black Monk's Pill before they stopped.

There was no chance to explain the King was not the King but only Fred E. Williams. There was no time even for a struggle. The instant the door opened and they leaned forward to scramble out, Angelo coshed them both.

Obie went down flat. My father still had a bit of spunk left in him to try and tell them who he was. He struggled to cling on to consciousness, scared he might be shipped off to some waiting boat if they thought he was the King. Then what would happen? Trussed and thrown overboard when they discovered their mistake? He raised his arm to try and tug on Angelo's black shirt, mumbling "I'm Fred. I'm Fred."

The renegades stared at him. All in one split second, Angelo turned with fury and began to beat on him. Emrys leapt into the fray crying, "What the bloody hell you doing, mate?" trying to intercept Angelo's vicious punches.

All to no avail. A blow landed fair and squarely on my father's nose. He felt the excruciating pain, the crunch of bone, the blood pouring from his nostrils. His eyes stung, almost too much to see. He heard Emrys shouting, "Bloody traitor," sensed him raise his good right arm and stick and wallop Angelo across the upper torso. My father tried to get up, to join the fight, but Angelo must have realised his plans were ruined. While Emrys panted for breath, Angelo hopped into the van and drove away. Tich chased after him, blarting like a stuck pig not to be left behind. And then – the lights went out.

There, in the greenhouse, with my father, immersed in what he told me, I croaked, "Dear God, Our Dad, he might have murdered you. Fancy Emrys coming through like that."

"Miracles will never cease. He laid us by the hedge and went to find out how to get us out of there. He never said he was contrite, but his deeds spoke reams. He found out that no buses ran that way. We'd have to walk. By and by, when we revived, and he had cleaned us up a bit, we started home. Emrys went ahead and brought the lads to help us over the last stretch."

He fell into a gentle reverie, sitting on his old three-cornered stool beside the stove. With his bent-tip poker he raked the ash abstractedly, our Nip's head on his knee.

If I was relieved he hadn't joined the gallery of national rogues, I was sorry that his heroism would go unrecorded. He ranked as high as Wales's bravest: Caradoc holding off the Romans, Owain Glyndŵr against the English, and a score more we paid tribute to on the feast of Dewi Sant.

He looked like one who, having faced a hard decision, knows he made the right and selfless choice. Still, there was a hint of sadness in his damaged face. I said, "There's too bad bang should go your chance again, Dad. The March, the telephone, and now the Kingnap Plot. It is a shame."

He made a grimace of resigned regret. "Yes. I would have liked to have dangled your little nipper on my knee one day, and told him how his Granddad was the King of England for a quarter of an hour back in 1936."

"So, in a sense, you were."

He brightened. "Aye. So, in a sense, I s'pose I was."

"It's a grand old story you'll have to tell," I said "And there's this bit for a happy ending." I told him then how I'd gone up to Blaenavon and caught the King's eye just before his saying, "Something must be done. Something will be done!" Then again with greater emphasis, "Something must and *will* be done."

"He said that, did He?" His face was like a day in June.

He repeated the words slowly, savouring them. "We haven't got Him wrong. He's a young man yet. A whole long reign in front of Him. In next to no time He'll be by this way again." He gained momentum. "I'll back my shirt it will be around his Coronation." The *hwyl* was on him; he was in full sail. "Now there's a bloody thought." A new edition of his mumpy glinted in his eye.

In spite of his discomfort and disfigurement, my father was in high old humour for the next few days. Even getting down the bath on bath-night from where it hung beside the coal-house door, was the occasion for a bit of waggery about the way we "lived like kings". A story was going around about the King, on his first night in South Wales, in Usk, sending to the town for a zinc bath. It had been delivered to the Royal Train parked in a siding.

My father revelled in the hornet's nest which the royal tour stirred up. The Tory press charged that the King's remarks, "Something must be done. Something will be done," was playing politics, which was constitutionally forbidden to the monarchy. It was even rumoured that the Government was so incensed, it was trying to stop the King's next scheduled tour. They didn't want him going to Tyneside, another depressed area, for fear he'd "interfere".

Other Conservative newspapers, however, like the *Daily Mail* and *Daily Express,* who clamoured for decisive leadership against the vacillating Baldwin, contrasted the King's energetic concern with the Government's flabbiness.

The Liberal and Labour views were adequately expressed by our own Bob Miller. He spoke bluntly at the Council meeting the following week. He was not only upset that the children didn't have a good look at the King, he said, he was disgusted at a lot of silly, uninformed criticism going round the district directed against the wrong people. It wasn't their fault, locally, that the King hadn't seen the things he should. He, Bob Miller, had personally asked the King to walk through the village. But Sir Samuel Hoare said time would not permit. Furthermore, he, Bob Miller, was very sorry that the King's name had been brought into party politics. The King was above party politics, and he hoped the people had the common sense to realise it.

My father's geniality helped members of the Loyal Order

to transform their disappointment into satisfaction. He lost no time selling them the next installment of his mumpy. They now had another "something to look forward to" – the Coronation Interview.

I would normally have revelled in my father's upbeat mood, but I had to turn my mind to other things. At the beginning of the school year I had gone up to fourth form. Many of the girls I started out with had peeled off, left school, gone to fill such jobs as shop assistants, clerks and mill hands. Being one of the ones still in the school system with my parents' backing and doing well in most subjects, I was scheduled to have a talk with my form mistress about future plans.

"What would you like to be, Davidia, when you leave school?" Miss Lawrence asked.

"I don't know, Miss. I haven't thought."

"It's time you did. You have to start deciding whether you will go into fifth form and matriculate. If so, it is not too soon to consider a career, and what higher education you may need. Do you hope to train for teaching or nursing?"

Either alternative alarmed me. "Oh, Miss, is that all?"

"What else do you have in mind? A secretary? Not a hairdresser."

"I could be an MP or on the Council."

Her eyes screwed into me over her half glasses. "No you couldn't. That is not a occupation. You wouldn't be a suitable candidate, in any case. You are a girl. You are a . . . You don't have the necessary background . . . or social qualities."

"I could try."

"It is not a bread and butter job. Do you want to fail in life? Who is going to keep you when you leave home? You need a profession or a trade. Politics is something for your spare time, if at all. Use a little common sense, Davidia. Think about it. Come back before breaking up for Christmas."

I did think about it. Miss Lawrence's utter dismissal made me feel a fool. I didn't want to starve. I didn't want to fail and end up on the dole. I might settle for teaching as the least obnoxious option. But it wasn't anything I wanted to deal with for a long time yet, let alone before we broke up for the Christmas holiday.

As a distraction from such worries, I pieced together what became of Angelo. Vowles's van was found abandoned near the docks. A week or so later, I happened into Lanzo's. Mrs. Lanzo mutely handed me a letter post-marked Naples and signed "Angelo". Ben translated it for me.

Angelo excused himself for leaving in a hurry. He had seized the chance to work his passage home. We figured out how he could have managed that. The first coal boat since the lifting of League sanctions against Italy had just left the Alexandra Dock. They must have signed him on.

The letter went on to say that he was shortly off to Spain to aid the Franco Nationalist insurgents in the Spanish Civil War. He ended ominously, "P.S. Tell Emrys if I see him there, I'll pay him what I owe him."

The much-chastened Emrys had made himself scarce around the village. My father put things straight for him by pointing out he had come to his senses in time to save the day. I ran into him in Lanzo's once. He was making plans to leave his Mam at last. Picking up Angelo's dare, he was going to Spain to join the Loyalists. I put it to him bluntly that with his gammy leg and arm he wouldn't be much good to them. But he said his pigeons would.

"Obie dealt with Tich, the little tyke," my father filled me in. "Put the fear of God in him, he did. *Twp* he is. Witless. Like his father. We shall have to put a clamp on him to keep him straight."

One other little item put a finishing touch to the scratched plot of the Kingnapping. In view of all the trouble with the plumbing, and the glaring eyesore it had proved on such a ceremonial occasion, the Council voted to tear down the urinal.

If the razing of that structure made a fitting ending to the local saga, the demise of another notorious edifice had a similar effect on the national level. The sudden destruction by fire of that glass-and-steel extravagance, Victoria and Albert's Crystal Palace, was judged "the ending of an era" in British history.

People like my mother said it spelled the end of the good, clean principles established by Queen Victoria. "You two scoundrels can mock me all you want to," my mother reproved us for our grins. "You are the living proof of the moral rot that have set in."

If my father and I had only known the "era" that would end in a day or two, I doubt we would have laughed so loud and hard. The joke was soon to be on us.

CHAPTER 20
DECEMBER 3 TO 10, 1936

The rest, as they like to say, is history. On December 3, not a fortnight after the visit to South Wales, came the news that the King desired to marry an American lady. She was twice divorced (the second husband not yet completely shed). It broke like a bombshell on the realm.

I wasn't present when my father first got wind of it. But I guessed he threw his cap down in the dust and stamped on it. I had seen him do this to his best trilby at a match where Wales got beaten.

As for myself, I learned the news from whisperings in the train on the way to school. Reggie Shatter claimed His Majesty was carrying on with some big-busted Hollywood blonde, and had got her in the family way. I couldn't say for sure, but I had a strong suspicion the story Emrys Strong had circulated earlier was nearer the truth. The American clippings in the leaflet I had caught my father reading early in November gave her class.

As soon as I got home, I devoured the *Daily Herald*. "A constitutional crisis of grave character has developed as a consequence of serious differences between the King and Cabinet." Mr. Harold Laski explained that if the King should scorn the Cabinet's advice, the Government would fall. Then the King would have to try to form a new one of ministers who shared his view and could command a majority in Parliament.

The question was: Could the King find the necessary parliamentary backing to marry Mrs. Simpson as he wished?

I was smart enough to wonder whether this meant Labour's chance to take the reins.

My father came home early complaining of a "red-hot poker stabbing in my guts." He chucked his tea-jack in the bosh, chipping the enamel. He slammed his food can on the draining board hard enough to warp the lid. He bumped the supper table till the china rattled. To make him even touchier, there were kippers for his supper. He took one impatient stab at trying to separate the teaspoonful of meat from its enormous skeleton of hairlike bones, and hurled it on the fire. Appalled at such a wicked sin, my mother rescued it with the fire tongs, swilled off the ash and cinder at the tap, and put it outside on the bailey for our Nip.

My father lit a cigarette and paced the coconut matting. "So help me God, they are out to tear him limb from limb, them bloody Scribes and Pharisees. It isn't the woman that brought it on. That's only an excuse. It is to pay him back and shut his gob for what they said was dabbling in politics. Take that bloody bishop telling him to smarten up his ways – the Church and Cabinet are all in league, the bloody rogues."

"You're wrong. It *is* the woman, Fred," my mother finally spoke up. "I would hate *my* kids to have to look up to a Queen like that. A mere nobody. Some common piece who has no conception of what holy matrimony is. Let alone the ways of majesty."

"Narrow and bigoted like all the flaming rest, you are." And the battle was engaged.

The next few hours their irreconcilable philosophies bumped heads over issues of Divorce, Public Duty versus Private Rights of Sovereigns, Americans. Each flung their total armoury of well-worn arguments into the fray. My father did achieve one novel thrust. "I suppose you'd rather that he made a bloody formal, loveless match to a Royal piece, and keep *this* woman on the side. Like some other

Kings not very long ago, not mentioning no names. You want to penalize him for his honour and decency to want to make an honest woman of the one he loves. I don't know why you women don't rally to her side for your own sake, if not for hers."

My mother was impregnable. "Don't put me in *her* class. Who is she? Some cheap peroxide blonde, no doubt. Loud and brazen. No corsets to hold her in respectable. All the American women down the pictures look like that. That's why I won't go."

Yet when Mrs. Simpson's picture appeared in the newspapers the following day (the day she fled to France) my mother sniffed, "Not much to look at, is she? Almost dowdy you might say. Sort of Plain-Jane-and-No-Nonsense with her thin lips and her hair pulled back severe like that. Whatever did he see in her? Wouldn't you have thought a King could do a little better than a mousy thing like her, the pick he has? She's not worth all this fuss. Good Lord, she's only just like us. You won't catch me bending *my* knee and humbling myself to her."

My father didn't bother to lambast her illogical contrariness. As he cut the rind off some bacon rashers and set them in the pan already spitting on the coals, he offered a concession. "All right, then. Don't let's make her Queen. Let the King marry her in some other capacity. Say as the Duke of Cornwall. That would be the only title she would get. A private marriage, nowt to do with us." It was clearly a compromise solution he had read somewhere to appeal to chauvinists like her. They called it "morganatic" marriage, a new word for us.

"And stop us ever having a real Queen to look up to while Edward is alive?" my mother bridled. "Unless you are proposing the King should commit bigamy."

With a sharp shake of his head I saw my father write my

mother off as a bad loss. He would waste no more time on her. With the crisis rising to a rapid head, he had more important things to do than try to change her narrow mind. For, stating so clearly, as she usually did, the views of the blind, prejudiced majority, she showed him how urgent the situation was.

An emergency assembly of the Loyal Order had to be convened without delay. My father called shift meetings to discuss what could be done to help the King. If the people could be roused to pit their strength against the Tory Cabinet in the next few crucial days, the solution of a private marriage might be accepted as a compromise.

He hurried through his breakfast and was gone before I left for school. I wished I could have mooched that day. But I couldn't let my team down. A rounders match was scheduled with a rival house that afternoon.

I learned later they tossed around the idea of an instant March on London – whether to badger the Prime Minister or cheer the King was not made clear. My father failed to muster enough enthusiasm. One pound ten and six was all the treasury contained after the expenses of the Kingnap plot – nothing useful to be done with that.

There were sadder facts than that. A number of loyal members turned out not to be so loyal after all. Several of them felt "conscience-bound" to turn in their feathers. Under no circumstances could Twm Sion condone divorce. Bryn Thomas's father had tangled with a swaggering doughboy in 1917 and been anti-Yankee ever since. Perce Cook's bossy wife detested Edward VIII because he once said something disapproving about suffragettes; she made obscure use of this occasion to present Perce with an ultimatum: resign the Order or clear out for good. You could bet a tanner there had been lumpy throats and swimming eyes as these names were stricken from the rolls.

My father spent the weekend trying to shame or bully the rest of them into going out and around to rally popular support. He coached them to envision how the mumpy now must work the other way. The King had need of us now, as we had needed Him.

I went to chapel with my mother, more to nourish my curiosity than my soul. We sang ominous hymns like Joseph Parry's 'Merthyr Tydvil: Dies Ire, Day of Wrath': "Great God what do I see and hear? The end of things created." The minister's prayers were full of passionate intensity, asking for God's grace in time of trouble. Prayers for the Royal Family and the King. "God grant him wisdom to choose duty to his subjects over selfish appetites."

What my father attempted on the local scene, the powerful were doing on a national scale. *The Daily Mail*, the *Daily Express* and the *News Chronicle* gave wholehearted backing to the Sovereign. Churchill led the rally to the King's defence, trying with Beaverbrook to mobilize sufficient opposition to bring down the Government. But he had the bad luck to attract support from unwelcome quarters: from the British Fascist Party's Sir Oswald Mosley, Communist Harry Pollitt, and a few other fringe groups in British politics.

It was one thing to learn on Monday that the morganatic marriage compromise was unacceptable to the arrogant Baldwin Government. It was quite another to take in the unbelievable news that the Labour Party backed Mr. Baldwin solidly. My father couldn't believe his eyes and ears. He was a man in shock, as though the trees had turned black overnight or Twn Barlum had vanished from our skyline on Mynydd Maen.

Labour's incredible misalliance with the Tories meant that the royal morganatic issue was doornail dead. On Labour's back rested the ultimate blame for leaving the King only two stark alternatives: the woman or the throne. But my father didn't see at once the inexorable trend of this devastating action. It took several more desperate days for its implications to sink in.

Local alignments and events continued to parallel the national scene. My father struggled valiantly to swing support towards his "twin". He went from shop to club to pub, from door to door, talking, talking, bright-eyed, earnest-tongued, putting everything he had in it.

But he couldn't crack the shell of high-and-mightiness. There was a touch of cruelty in their severity to see the highest leveled in the dust. A getting-even glee. My sister Muriel reported after a visit to the cinema, "When they showed the newsreel of the King's visit to South Wales, I was the only one who clapped. I did feel small." By time we got it, the news was always history.

The blow of Labour's betrayal on the national scene was nothing to the blow my father suffered when his closest butties followed suit. "Sorry, Fred," said Obie. "I stand with Attlee. The King can't have the penny and the bun." My father scoffed, "What does a toff like Attlee know about the likes of us."

Nwd said, "Give in, Fred. You are burning yourself out. It en no use. The Baldwin bunch have won."

"That isn't true. No vote's been taken yet. Still no debate. This hush-hush is a trick to make us pack it in. I am the last to back old Churchill. But he's right. There is no sense to rush it. We all need time. They are trying to ram it down our throats." He pounded his fists against his forehead. "If only Lloyd George had been here in the country when it started." Lloyd George, the great Welsh Prime Minister of World War I, had just published his war memoirs. "He'd never have let it get this far. He wouldn't have allowed the secrecy. The Americans knew everything three months ago." But Lloyd George was far away when he was needed, in Jamaica, halfway across the world, with his other lady.

What my father needed was a mouthpiece for his own special, singular opinions. He suffered horribly from his inability to communicate, to influence the outcome. Newspapers and the radio transmitted their opinions and those of the rich and powerful loudly and almost instantaneously. Democracy gave simple citizens no equal channel for expression.

Even those members of the Loyal Order who stayed loyal had lost their fight. They were like a clog around my father's leg. "We've got to get Arthur Jenkins and Nye Bevan to press for time to put in our opinions," he begged his butties.

Ted Swilling said, "Delay ent good, Fred. Hitler eyes us like a hawk. If not to pounce on *us* then on someone else. Why else is Mosley fanning it?"

Each resignation from the Loyal Order was a knife twist in my father's heart. He could not bear to think that his life-long mumpy could come to this, or believe his butties would betray the name and nature of their Order.

By Tuesday evening, December 8, that once-glorious brotherhood had shrunk to a number you could count upon one hand. The remnants were a sad assortment. Barney was still in. The official Catholic line favoured the re-establishment of the monarchy as an active force in government. So it saw fit, ironically, to turn a blind eye to Mrs. Simpson's previous marriages. The equally ironic pro-King line of the Communist Party kept Emrys in. Leonard Hasty stayed because he and our Muriel were incurable romantics. And Uncle Jack stayed not to break my father's heart.

My father steadfastly refused to recognize the morganatic issue dead. If the choice had narrowed to an either/or, he knew, as surely as he knew himself, which course the King would choose – a bleak reality my father could not stand to face. He clung to the belief that the good sense of the British people would ultimately prevail so the King could have his love, and we could have the King.

On Wednesday, December 9, I found my father nailing strips of wood together. I watched in silence as he linked the frames with webbing. I guessed he planned to wear the boards suspended from his shoulders like Dan, Dan, the Sandwich Man, a walking poster through the Newport Streets. The legends on my father's posters read: "Down with Baldwin! God Save the King!" And on the other side: "Rise up for Edward. Give him his Lady. Keep us our King."

He planned to walk to Pontypool and back that evening. I went along with him but kept my distance to the rear; he made me feel a bit ashamed. His eccentricity apart, he looked a sketch. There was a quiet madness in his eyes and a cadaverous look about his hairy face. He still had sticking plaster on his nose.

But I wouldn't have dreamt of trying to talk him out of it. It was better for him to stay active than to brood. In any case, there was no stopping him. Though his voice rasped and his breath came hard, he would fight until he dropped. As he hiked, he shouted out remarks to passers-by, "Let the King know you are on his side. Don't let the top dogs throw him to the wolves. You are letting them dictate and force our hand."

A raggle-taggle bunch of snot-nosed kids ran after him yelling, "Hark the Herald Angels Sing, Mrs. Simpson vamps our King." Others used him as a target for their slings and pea-shooters. Even the most innocent made faces, thumbed their noses or stuck out their tongues as he went by.

At a street corner in Sebastapol where a lot of seedy customers hung around, he stopped to make a soapbox speech. "Are you going to let them nail Him to the cross? What has He done, poor bugger, except fall in love?"

A slattern woman with greasy ropes of hair, oozing breasts and a beer-barrel stomach, heckled, "She en nothing but a bleeding trollop. *Ach a fi!*"

My father fixed her with a scathing look. "You be Maude Rawlings, bent you. Aye, aye, then, you can shout, seeing you live in a glass house yourself."

She spat at him as ribald laughter drove her off.

He took on other hecklers. He branded as "gutter talk" the charges of the King's pro-fascist bent. "That's treason, mate. The man you're speaking evil of is King of England. You ought to be run in." He shook his fist at them.

The foulness of the catcalls, the sly pushing of the crowd, their ugly grimaces, alarmed me. I was glad a bobby came to break it up. Even so, I saw no reason he should be so snotty to my father – as my father, "with all due respect," told him in so many words.

"If you don't watch out, I'll take you in," the bobby growled.

I put in hastily, "Come on, our Dad. Let's shove. There is too much to be done to waste time here," and, as I like to think, saved him from a flare of temper and a night in gaol.

I left him when I knew my mother would be worrying about my whereabouts. When I got home I told her, "Don't wait up for him."

"What's he up to now?"

I fibbed, "There is an urgent meeting for the King. He will be late." The less she knew the better of the sandwich board parade and his street corner oratory. She would be mortified and nag him ragged. Now was not the time for lecturing.

I heard him come home after midnight. It was a long time after that he came to bed. He must have sat before a dead fire in the bitter cold. The wind blew off the mountains from the north that night.

He was up and off to work next morning, on six-till-two

shift, the same as usual. He came into my room before he left. His face looked pasty under a two-or-three-day growth of tawny beard.

He said, "Vid, here is a couple of bob. And a telegram I've wrote for you to send. Don't tell your Mam, she'll only worry. Send it from somewhere on your way to school. You know these busybodies down the village quizzing into everybody's business. You'll do this for me, will you, love? There's a good kid. I knew you would." He squeezed my shoulder. "You are my rock," he said.

He had printed neatly: "TO KING EDWARD VIII FORT BELVEDERE. WE NEED A WORD FROM YOUR MOST GRACIOUS MAJESTY. YOUR SILENCE A LOT THINK IS FUNNY. SPEAK TO THE PEOPLE ON THE WIRELESS. THEY WILL RALLY WHEN THEY HEAR YOUR VOICE. WE ARE WITH YOU TO THE DEATH. SIGNED FRED WILLIAMS, PRESIDENT, LOYAL ROYAL ORDER OF THE PRINCE OF WALES."

The girl who counted up the words stared at me as if a hole gaped where my brains should be. It meant being late for school, but I got it sent.

CHAPTER 21

That afternoon, Thursday, December 10, the King's Message of Intent to Abdicate was read in the House of Commons.

My father wasn't in when I got home. I dared not ask my mother where he was for fear of setting her off fretting. We stuck close to the wireless, scarcely speaking all that evening. We listened avidly to the story that the Prime Minister at last unfolded of what went on behind the scenes since the middle of October.

The whole thing was an eye-opener. What made me sit up straight particularly was the fact the King had stated his irrevocable intention of marrying Mrs. Simpson ("I am going to marry Mrs. Simpson, and am prepared to go") on November 16, <u>the night before he had visited South Wales</u>. So was "Something will be done" an empty promise? I wondered how things might have gone if my father and his co-conspirators had only known.

A bit more candidness on Mr. Baldwin's part might at least have saved my father all the pain and suffering of yesterday. Even as he had exposed himself to ridicule, and gone sleepless, frozen, composing his poignant telegram in his last, desperate effort to swing the battle, and even as I wasted his two shillings that could have gone towards the new overcoat he needed, it had been too late. The King had already come to terms with destiny.

My mother was preparing the mixture for the Christmas puddings for boiling next day in the copper. While she chopped suet, stoned raisins, sliced citron peel and candied fruit, and crushed lumps out of the demarera sugar with a rolling pin, she found time to interject such harsh remarks as, "Stubborn fool. You'd think a king would have more sense.

"Fancy giving up a throne and country for a tart. I don't think much of anybody who puts love or fancy before duty. We are well shot of him if that's the sort he is. That poor Mr. Baldwin had something to put up with, by the sound of it. The King did not deserve to have it handled with so much discretion."

I was glad my father didn't have to hear her gibes. They would have flailed him raw. But it worried me to imagine how he must be taking it. I wondered where he was.

Our Muriel came home at seven. She had forfeited her half-day off to help Mrs. Pattimore stick balls of cotton wool spelling "Merry Christmas" on the windows, and put sprigs of holly around the shelves. That such superficialities could still go on in the face of ominous events bewildered me.

As soon as our Mu came in, she said, "Where is Our Dad, then?"

"God knows," my mother said. "He barely picked his dinner, that morbid was he. I was glad to see the back of him. It is unbelievable how cross and snarly he's been lately. If I am hindered doing this job any more, the puddings won't have time to ripen. Your Nana liked to let them ripen for six weeks and more."

"I wonder how he's taking it?" my sister said.

"Indeed, I wonder. I expect he'll sulk a bit."

By keeping mum, I hoped to stay up till my father came. But noticing the time at last, she shooed me off to bed. When I went to peck her cheek goodnight, she said, "He is a devil. He knows I worry. I hope he is all right."

I was wide-awake and wondering when our Muriel came up. I still hadn't closed my eyes when my mother climbed the stairs. The middle kitchen clock struck twelve.

"Viddy, love," she whispered, coming through my door. "Are you awake?"

"Aye, Mam."

"I am worried where your Dad is."

"I expect he is all right."

"It is not like him to be so late unless he lets me know."

"Drowning his sorrows, I wouldn't doubt," I jested to relieve her, risking getting him in worse.

"The pubs are closed this long time. The club an hour gone."

"Aye, but you know what he is. He's very likely arguing outside of one of them."

"I s'pose." But anxiety still lapped at her. I knew I couldn't talk her out of it. It was sloshing round, contaminating me as well.

"Do you think I ought to go along the bank and see?" I said.

That did it. With its associations of suicides and drownings, references to the canal bank raised hackles in the dead of night. I knew better than to mention it, but it just slipped out. I even scared myself.

There would be no rest for either of us now until I went and checked.

I scoured the village first, with emphasis on pubs and clubs. Then I circled around the road to the bridge between the "first" and "second" banks of the canal. I combed the area back towards the house and then retraced my steps to search beyond the bridge.

It must have been a sixth sense that made me look inside of Bowkert's gate up by Five Locks.

There I found him, lying on the ground.

His placards were beside him, blurred and mucked. "God Save the King. Nobody else will."

And he, dead drunk. Well, no, not quite. With prodding and persuasion, I roused and raised him. Twigs and leaves stuck to his cheek and hair. I brushed them off.

I don't know how I got him home. There was only half a mile to go. But every other step we had to stop for him to retch his heart up in the reeds. I dragged and pushed him all the way.

When I got him home he wanted to go in the shed – which was as well. I didn't want my mother seeing him like that. Scolding was the last thing that he needed. He had drunk himself into insensibility because he was beside himself.

I went to tell my mother we were home. Fear left her face and softness washed her eyes. All she said was, "Drink will be the death of him."

"You go to bed, our Mam. I'll keep him company till he is more himself. Then I'll bring him in to doss down on the sofa."

She touched my cheek. "You are a good girl. Better than a son to him."

My father had revived a bit when I returned with our Nip at my heels. He was sitting on the floor, leaning on a sack of powdered sheep manure. Nip licked his hand, and he stroked him absent-mindedly. "It must have been some bad beer I got down me. Some pub up near Pontymoile." Making excuses for himself, he couldn't be so bad. Though his tongue was thick and slurring still.

"Nobody will blame you, our Dad. What with the blasted news."

The red rims round his eyes got redder. His nostrils twitched. It would be good for him to have it out. Not push him, let him take his own sweet time.

So that he wouldn't feel embarrassed by my watching him, I busied myself scrubbing pots that had been soaking in a bucket.

"Bloody fools," he said. "The public. Sucked in. Flaming idiots."

"I agree with you."

He shuffled around, feeling in his pockets in slow motion. He fetched out a sixpence and stretched it up to me.

"What's this for?" I said offhandedly.

"For being a good kid. Looking after your old Dad." His lips were quivering.

I pocketed the sixpence without any fuss. I started tidying up the mess left on his workbench since he threw the sandwich boards together.

After a while he said, "You know what scuttled the poor bugger, Vid? Secrecy. That's right. Secrecy. That's what scuttled the poor bugger, Vid."

"That's right," I said, encouraging him to have his head. Behind his bleary eyes and dopey, dribbling mouth, his mind was clear.

"By keeping it hush-hush, they bullied Him into thinking that he only had two choices: the woman or the throne. But what kind of choice is that, mun? Hobson's choice." He had his arguments down pat. He'd been making them for days. "Would us have been rejoicing here this night if He had chucked the woman like a bloody cad? What price duty then? Could we have looked up to a King who left his loved ones in the lurch?"

He had a point. I told him so.

"Crafty lot of flamers," he said vehemently, "throwing Him out, but making it look like He went of His own free will." He spat into a pile of rusty slag. Nip roused and settled back. "And I blame Labour more than I do Baldwin. Those questions Attlee put day after day were nothing but a put-up job."

The thought was so abrasive, it re-sparked the rage-light in his eyes. "It was Attlee's duty to have *forced* the truth into the open. Not play the Tories' games. All that claptrap Labour mouthed about defending the people's constitutional rights against the sovereign. It is a pity they didn't defend our constitutional rights *to know the truth* and make our voices heard. If they'd had any guts, they could have sent Baldwin packing, and formed a coalition with other back-benchers of the same mind. Kept the King and helped the working-man."

His mind was now so cutting sharp, so true, nobody would believe he'd been in such a state half an hour earlier. He stormed on, "But Labour is as blind and petty as the rest. How could they let so glorious a chance slip by? The likes won't come again for many a year. They have betrayed us all who put our faith in them." He spat again into the slag.

In a little bit he started up again to his audience of one. "This abdication proves our damn democracy is not the open book it is supposed to be. The whole world knew before we did. Americans laughing up their flaming sleeves. No better are we than the bloody Germans or the Russians the way they keep the truth from us."

"I know," I said. "To think the King made up his mind before he came down here. The day before!" The irony intrigued me. "I wonder what you would have done if you had known?"

Old mouthy me! No sooner had I said it than I knew I'd put my foot in it. He sucked his breath in sharply. He rubbed his hands over his face as though to wash pervading pain away. "There is the shit of it," he said. "We *did* know. I was one of the few buggers Baldwin *didn't* have it secret from."

"But Dad, you didn't know if Emrys's old rumour rag was true or not!"

"I did. You know the way I talked that I believed it in my heart." He pinched his mouth and pleated his brows to fight the anguish gripping him. "There was that dream as well.

The men in black with sheep crooks after him. My heart knew they were hounding him. His enemies."

"Supposing for the sake of argument you *did* know all. What difference did it make?"

"What difference?! All the difference in the world. The only reason that the people didn't go for morganatic marriage was they never got a chance to hear His side of it. Nor time to think it through . . . Why do you think that crooked Baldwin kept Him gagged and prisoner in that bloody Fort? Not far short of condemning a man without a trial. Or torturing a confession out of him."

I stood there with my mouth wide open. He urged me, "Don't you see, Vid? He needed somebody to go to bat for Him. Force the whole situation into the open. Argue His side of the case. Only us, the Loyal Order, could have done it for him." He drove his clenched fist hard against his thigh. "If we had only had an ounce of selflessness in us, we should have gone on with our Kingnap Plot, the risks be damned. Not for *our* sakes, but for *His*. Not to tell *our* grouses, but hark to *His*. Ask about the rumours and offer help. If the constitution wouldn't let the poor chap plead His own cause, we'd have done it for Him."

Suddenly my father's mumpy revealed its meaning. At last the prince and pauper were equal – in defeat. Two naively trusting souls, identical in need, identically thwarted – both urgent to be heard, both rendered voiceless – were now put down, undone, by powerful forces who made a travesty of constitutional democracy. These spiritual twins who had brushed past each other in the dark without ever touching were exiled now forever from each other.

My father was talking still, what-iffing now as though to keep despair at bay. "Oh, what a pact we could have made to help each other. Foxed that crafty Baldwin and that coward Atlee. Broken the conspiracy of silence of the press, the government, and opposition. We'd have spread the news up and down this land. Oh, what a marvelous case we would have made for Him. For Us. For us and Him."

There was nothing to be said. I could have argued till the banishment of want how how slim this chance had been of bringing off the Kingnap Plot. And even if they had, what a next-to-hopeless job it would have been to organize a rally to the King. My father would have answered me that it didn't matter what the odds were, they would have triumphed in the end. And with that kind of faith, perhaps no obstacle was insurmountable.

I watched the dream and zeal fade from his eyes, and reality rush in. He said, "But no, I didn't give one stinking, paltry little thought to Him. I was too wrapped up in self. All me and mine. Some fellow spirit to King Edward VIII Fred Williams have proved hisself." His self-contempt was devastating. He was convinced beyond dissuasion he had failed his King.

He said, "Oh Vid. The weight of guilt and blame hangs heavy in me here." He thumped his chest. "I let him down. I have failed Him when He needed me. What a bloody friend I am."

"No, no. That isn't true. How many times have you told me there's no shame in not succeeding if you tried your best."

If I could have found the words I would have told him, however daft his mumpy, it came out of his passion to bring justice to the common man. He would go on failing, being defeated, and he would still roll upright, like a weighted doll. His will was everything.

And I saw with washed eyes, my life through his. I knew what I was going to tell Miss Lawrence – despite her predictions of my failure I was sticking to my dream. If I saw something must be done, I would do it and accept the consequences, though I might fail and fail again. Our freedom to keep challenging failure is our one enduring success.

I led him down the house. I got him on the sofa. I unlaced his boots and pulled them off. I signalled our Nip to cwtch up to him and keep him warm. I fetched the flannel from the sink and wiped his cheeks clean of dried vomit, dirt and tear tracks. I put a cushion underneath his head, and threw an overcoat across his legs. I patted him. The poor old sod was inconsolable.

Well, there it is. Even a grown man was entitled to a good old weep for the shattering of a cherished mumpy that failed to make a dent in history.

7|04

ABOUT HONNO

Honno Welsh Women's Press was set up in 1986 by a group of women who felt strongly that women in Wales needed wider opportunities to see their writing in print and to become involved in the publishing process. Our aim is to publish books by, and for, women of Wales, and our brief encompasses fiction, poetry, children's books, autobiographical writing and reprints of classic titles in English and Welsh.

Honno is registered as a community co-operative and so far we have raised capital by selling shares at £5 a time to over 400 interested women all over the world. Any profit we make goes towards the cost of future publications. We hope that many more women will be able to help us in this way. Shareholders' liability is limited to the amount invested, and each shareholder, regardless of the number of shares held, will have her say in the company and a vote at the AGM. To buy shares, to buy books directly, to be added to our database of authors or to receive further information about forthcoming publications, please e-mail: post@honno.co.uk or write to Honno:

'Ailsa Craig',
Heol y Cawl,
Dinas Powys,
Bro Morgannwg
CF64 4AH.

www.honno.co.uk